# A Crofter's Tale

## (The REAL Story behind the Hartlepool Monkey Legend)

**Gareth McArtur & Andre Boulanger**

A Crofter's Tale (The REAL Story of The Hartlepool Monkey)

# Preface

There have been many takes on the Hartlepool Monkey tale. Stories passed down through the years about how the locals of Hartlepool found a washed up monkey on the headland after a storm, around the time of the Napoleonic War. Having never seen such a beast before they naturally assumed the animal to be a spy for the filthy French and promptly hanged him. Natives of Hartlepool have been cruelly labelled "Monkey hangers" ever since. Some are proud of the name. Many would rather forget the ignorance of their forefathers.

But what is the truth of the legend? There are some who believe the 'monkey' was actually a boy – monkey being the term given to the unfortunate lad who had to shin up the mast to the crow's nest and act as a lookout – however, if they'd seen a boy, surely, even in those savage and lawless times, their natural instincts would have been to save the life?

The authors of this book have conducted tireless research into the legend and have uncovered some remarkable facts which prove beyond reasonable sense that, far from being a spy, the beast which landed on the headland that stormy night was a most coveted specimen. It was indeed a simian. A simian worth so much more than as a tool for espionage. A simian so rare that it's like had been pursued for hundreds of years by a mysterious order whose sole purpose was to capture and seize the special powers it held and utilise them for its own evil intent.

The tale they have uncovered reveals the real reason for the monkeys sorry end at the hands of his unwitting killers and leads us on a frightening journey of discovery. Set in modern times the story begins with an unwelcome visitor.....

## Chapter One

### *"The Unwelcome Visitor....!"*

The rain lashed against the windowpane, jettisoned by the wind so that it powered into the glass as if trying to break it, demanding to be let in, imploring the occupants of the smart, but hideously over priced, South London town house to give it shelter from itself.
No chance of that. Warm and cosy by the roaring fireside sat David and Julia Snaith. David with his night-cap, a small brandy, and Julia, in her fluffy 'Holiday Inn' dressing gown, with a steaming mug of hot cocoa. Had Julia known that her future husband wore a night-cap she might have revised her answer to his proposal. They'd been married for just three weeks and were just back from their honeymoon. The young couple snuggled together as if trying to shut themselves off from the tempest that raged outside. The more they tried to shut out the noise the louder it became until it seemed as if their shiny new house would crumble around them. David was scared and Julia did her best to comfort him, whilst at the same time hiding her own growing unease. They'd never lasted this long. Storms were not usually the norm in southern England, especially after such a long cool spring, but this one had lasted all afternoon and evening. Every type of weather imaginable had been thrown from the skies. Hail, sleet, wind, rain, thunder, lightning; and now the combination of gale force wind and heavy, almost tropical, rain appeared as though it would tear down their house with all the ferocity of a hurricane.

# A Crofter's Tale (The REAL Story of The Hartlepool Monkey)

In spite of the rain and wind the couple eventually began to drift into a light sleep, David stirring occasionally, his dozing interrupted by the destructive force outside, until neither of them could resist the onset of deep relaxing, refreshing slumber.

*Crack!!* David woke first, startled by the loud noise. Julia stirred. "Don't worry David. It was just a tin can or something hitting the window. Go back to sleep." she said, drowsily.

"What if a roof tile's comes off or something, it's bad enough to blow the whole bloody roof off anyway; I'd best go and check. Will you come with me?" he asked, touching her shoulder gently. She brushed his hand away,

"No. Now stop fussing and go back to sleep."

David sighed and went to investigate alone.

A black shape shifted in the corner of the smartly decorated lounge. At precisely the same time as a flash of blue lightning illuminated the room.

"What the f...?" David's words were lost in the hideous scream that drowned out all of the ensuing noise. The scream didn't come from David, or his again sleeping wife. The scream that had ripped the words from David's mouth came from the vile creature across the room. The creature shifted again, and this time David could make out some of the features of the beast, it was big, too big to be a human. It screamed again. A guttural growl followed and then it revealed itself into the flickering glow of the dying fire. David was horrified to see a soaking, sobbing baboon before him.

"Julia!" he yelled.

The baboon was growling pitifully and holding something in his right hand. David could just make out a dark liquid oozing from the animal's clenched fist. He instinctively knew that it was blood. A flash of neon blue from the electric storm outside highlighted the pained and angry expression on the baboon's face. It softened slightly as he recognised the fear and pity in David's manner. It held out the bloodied hand and slowly opened it to reveal a small, nutmeg shaped orb. The mangled orb glistened with blood. Was it an eye? David thought to himself. No, the creature clearly had two of those, both seeping huge baboon tears. From nowhere a voice screamed.

"It's his left testicle David! Look!"

David spun round to see his wife pointing at the baboon's groin. He quickly switched on the light – the room instantly ablaze with bright yellow light.

"Sie ist richtig!" said the baboon.

"My God!" gasped Julia, "It's German…!"

"What?" bellowed her bewildered husband.

"He….erm, it's German!" she once again exclaimed.

It appeared to David that his wife was perhaps in shock otherwise why would she make such a ridiculous statement. Trying to compose himself he gently, but assertively, whispered "Calm down dear" (in a manner not dissimilar to those awful Michael Winner insurance adverts on television).

"I'm telling you David, that thing is German, or at least he's speaking German."

"How do you know?" said David.

"I remember a small amount of German from School." she responded. Julia went on to explain that although she had despised language lessons at school, most of all German (in the main due to a bombastic teacher by the name of Mr Martlew) she had managed to remember a small number of words and phrases. She further explained that on one of the very rare occasions that she was asked a question, which she was expected to respond to in German, she had got the question right and the teacher had responded by saying "Sie ist richtig" *("She is right")*.

"Oh," said David sarcastically. "Well that's just bloody marvellous."(equally sarcastically). "Aren't you more concerned with the fact we have a haemorrhaging simian in our home? I know I am. He could do anything; I'll call the police!" he snapped.

"Nein!" yelled the rain soaked anthropoid.

# A Crofter's Tale (The REAL Story of The Hartlepool Monkey)

They turned their attentions back to the Baboon, stared open-mouthed and awaited its next movement or retort. They didn't have to wait too long. Once again the Baboon spoke.

"Sie ist richtig. I mean, she is right, but please don't call the police."

The Snaiths heads began to spin as this was becoming all too surreal.

"Ihre Frau ist richtig, ich bin Deutsch..err sorry, your wife is correct, I am German and I am indeed holding one of my testicles, though I have to admit I hadn't stopped to consider whether it was the right or the left one! Please, I mean you no harm." winced the baboon.

Having made this comment the Baboon peered down at his groin, gingerly poked and prodded at his wounded genitalia and found that the mangled orb he held in his right hand was hanging by the thinnest strand of epididymal tissue from the left side of his leaking loins. A clap of thunder almost drowned out his next response.

"Es ist mein linker Hode!" tears welled, and then fell from the baboon's eyes.

David, upon hearing the Baboon utter what he assumed to be more Germanic tongue, looked to his wife for linguistic translation/verification. However, Julia simply shrugged her shoulders.

"I wasn't that good at German." she admitted.

This time the Baboon helped out.

"You must forgive me." he said, almost apologetically. "I was just confirming that it is indeed the left testicle that is missing or rather that I'm holding in my bloodied hand."

No sooner had the Baboon finished his sentence (at this stage we have to assume the ape to be male, bloodied testicle notwithstanding, as stereotypes dictate that males are more adept at linguistics – though for the Snaiths' this stereotype seems to be

# A Crofter's Tale (The REAL Story of The Hartlepool Monkey)

somewhat inverted.) he staggered and fell to the floor with a crashing thud.

"David, do something!" urged Julia.

"What?" responded David.

"Weren't you in the St John's Ambulance Brigade when you were a teenager?"

"Yes, but we didn't practice on monkeys in those days, perhaps that's all changed now!" he snapped sarcastically.

"He's not a monkey, he's an ape!"[1] said Julia quite proudly.

"Why, I oughta!" mocked David (showing Julia the back of his hand – in a scene reminiscent of an old Three Stooges movie).

"Don't you raise your hand to me David Snaith, or I'll smash your face in. Just do something will you."

David approached the wretched creature and carefully, but with a degree of daring, examined the beast. First of all he looked the creature up and down and took in a large intake of breath. David had once aspired to be a car mechanic in his youth and this natural way of breathing, whilst simultaneously shaking the head back and forth stood him in good stead. Alas, his aspirations were dealt a cruel blow when he discovered, in his late teens that he was allergic to engine oil, petrol/diesel and all things automotive; and, if this wasn't bad enough, he later developed a phobia of all cars (with the exception of the Robin Reliant) but more of this later, perhaps. Anyway, the visual inspection served only to confirm what he already knew. This was an ape (not a monkey, look up the difference in a book or ask a Biology teacher[2]). He also knew that the ape was indeed German, as confirmed by both the ape itself and his wife. He gently touched the animal on the forehead (he'd seen this sort of thing on Casualty and/or E.R) and as he did the animal started to stir (in a fashion that would suggest it was coming round from an unconscious state, rather than the act of agitating a liquid i.e. tea/coffee/paint etc). The animal looked

---

[1] A

David in the eyes and muttered "Please, I must apologise, I appear to have made a rather nasty stain on your carpet".

"Shush!" comforted David. "This carpet has seen lots of stains in its life, I'm sure a little blood will do it no further harm."

"You don't understand." said the ape and pointed at his lower regions.

It then became clear. The Baboon had lost all control of its bodily function during its state of unconsciousness and defecated all over itself and the living room shag. The stench was, by now, noticeable and unbearable. However, both David and Julia (being both British and of stout constitution) ignored the mess and pretended they hadn't noticed, though David asked Julia to get him some rubber gloves.

Strangely, both David and Julia became more and more relaxed as events began to unfold. Their initial shock at seeing this mysterious bleeding simian (in terms of his haemorrhaging and not a derogatory slur) turned to sympathy and a desire to help the ailing anthropoid. David asked Julia to fetch some towels and hot water (again, this request was spurred by an episode of Holby City, though the episode in question was about a young girl who was about to give birth). Julia did as was requested and brought David the said articles. David began the process of cleaning the animal's wounds and stemming the flow of blood at the same time.
"Now for the tricky bit" he exclaimed. "Fetch the sewing kit I purloined from the hotel we were at last weekend" Again, Julia dutifully obeyed David and brought forward the tools he had so confidently and assertively requested. By now David looked as though he actually knew what he was doing and he proceeded to enthusiastically nip together the remains of the animal's scrotum with a length of green nylon thread. Within minutes he was done and so was the beast as on at least three or four occasions, during the procedure, he had again lapsed into unconsciousness.

Thankfully, it wasn't too long before the animal roused once more. The bleeding had also stopped. The 'operation' had been a success. Only time would tell if more serious complications would set in given that the whole procedure was done in a less than sterile environment (remember the faecal matter!).

"Would you like a drink? Tea, perhaps?" asked Julia.

"I'm an ape, we don't drink tea!"

"Of course!" replied Julia. "What about coffee?" she asked.

"That would be very nice, milk and two sugars please" requested the beast. Again, Julia dutifully obliged and went off to the kitchen to prepare the beverage. Upon her return she slipped upon one of the animals stools which served to upset the tray on which she was carrying the hot caffeine based beverages. Luckily for Julia she was able to restore her balance quickly and avert what would have been another unwelcome catastrophe. Rather, all that had happened was that a solitary fruit shortcake biscuit fell from the salver and onto the floor, nestling itself in close proximity (actually right on top) of one of the Baboon's turds. Julia, being the waste conscious person she was, quickly retrieved it and immediately offered it to her husband who, because he had not seen the near catastrophic incident, took the comestible and proceeded to greedily devour it (they are, after all, David's favourite).

"We must get a new biscuit tin Julia these biscuits are a little soggy". Julia smiled and agreed a new biscuit tin would go straight to the top of next weeks shopping list. The Baboon laughed. It was the first time he had done so since his unexpected arrival. David, oblivious to this, carried on feasting on his poo-based snack. Julia said nothing, looked at the Baboon and winked as if to suggest that this was their secret (the first of many they would share together).

A few minutes quickly sped by as they finished their refreshments. As the minutes passed the Snaiths' curiosity grew and grew and grew further. Curiosity, after a further minute or so grew into fully blown curiosity (and in the far distance several cats could be heard shuffling off their mortal coils), until finally the silence was broken. It was broken by the mysterious beast.

"Thank you, kind people. Please let me introduce myself". Although Julia's initial suspicions confirmed the ape to be German and indeed the animal itself affirmed her suspicions, he was now speaking in English. We can therefore assume the animal to be bi-lingual and need not delve into the reasons why or how he came to master two languages, let alone one!

"My name is Heinrich. Heinrich Himmler." An eruption of thunder punctuated the disclosure. Both David and Julia looked on amazed at what the animal had revealed.

"I admit my name is somewhat strange, if not disturbing, but let me assure you it is as equally accidental as it is co-incidental. For you see my parents, Adolf and Eva, are but simple folk and know nothing of social and political history nor are they aware of the concept of political correctness, irony and subtlety".

"Mein Got!" said David, then immediately anglicised his intended reaction, so as not to cause offence or indeed give the animal any reason to think he was in some way a fascist, by saying "My God, what an utterly incredible disclosure. How are you feeling Heinrich?"

"I'm much better thanks to you and your wife, but please call me Heinny, all my friends do." So shall it be proclaimed, David and Julia dutifully concurred.

"Me, David, this (pointing to his wife) Julia!" explained David.

"Surely you mean 'My name is David and this is my wife Julia'?" said the ape. David's thoughts quickly raced back to the Three Stooges and although he made gestures akin to the aforementioned 'Stooges' he did refrain from quoting the "Why I oughta!" line having realised that he was, after all, being a little condescending. Rather, David apologised as did Julia (in a spectacularly dutiful way).

"Now that we are on first name terms and we've established that you are comfortable following my first-aid like intervention perhaps you could tell me what you are doing here, and, more to the point, how did you get in?" asked David earnestly.

"Certainly" proclaimed Heinny. "I came in through the bathroom window as it was left open." David tutted at Julia.

"Don't look at me David, you're the security freak, you should have checked it." she glowered at him. The baboon continued,

"The tale that I'm about to relay to you is so chilling and so fantastic that it will send shivers down your spine and have you questioning your own sanity. You will also learn that I have sought out you good, kind people, to fulfil a long-held prophesy." The Snaiths listened with bated breath. All that mattered in their world, at this moment in time, now rested on what was about to come from the lips of this extraordinary anthropoid called Heinrich Himmler.

"My story begins with a hero, as all epic tales do." began Heinny.

"Who, who?" asked David.

"Be quite man, the ape is talking" barked Julia. David flinched at his wife's acid tongue and dutifully shut up to allow Heinny to continue.

"The hero's name is O'nad, Gerard O'nad......."

## Chapter Two

### *"Gerard O'nad"*

"Gerard O'nad was a simple Irish immigrant living in a small fishing town in the North-East of England, around about the end of the eighteenth century." began Heinny.

"He was well known to the locals who had nicknamed him 'Bollock', for reasons best known to themselves. He was also known for his inability to hold his drink, and was frequently found, standing in a pool of the local brew, having dropped his goblet yet again. O'nad was very rarely drunk."

Outside the wind swept by the still open bathroom window, for a second David thought he should go and close it. The thought was lost as the baboon continued.

"Conversely, the locals were in a perpetual state of drunken stupor, and were frequently found on the beach, foraging for tit-bits of food and drink washed up from the many shipwrecks which occurred along that stretch of rocky coast. These wrecks were usually caused by the locals themselves, in their perpetual stupor, forgetting to light the warning beacons."

"The locals, or Crofters as they were known, would rush to the sea front to save as many valuables as they could – usually exotic foods and fine wines - whilst ignoring the desperate pleas for help from their washed up crews."

Heinny paused for a while, as if trying to remember the rest of the tale, shifting uncomfortably in his chair. David and Julia sat together, both holding their breath, in a bated fashion.

"One very stormy night," he continued "an incident occurred which would have far reaching consequences for both the Crofters and our friend Mr O'nad. A German cargo ship fell victim to the rocks. The ship was crewed by eight of my forefathers and, alas, only one survived the impact, his name was Albert Himmler. Albert had sailed from Hamburg with a precious cargo of gold, diamonds and bratwurst to find a new life in Britain and escape the persecution being inflicted upon apes in his homeland."

"Sadly, it was not to be, for when the Crofters discovered his almost lifeless body they began to kick him violently. In a desperate bid for freedom Albert summoned all his strength to utter the words which would, cruelly, seal his fate. The only words of English he knew, taught to him by his grandmother who thought they would be useful in England, *'Ich kann, I.....can....make...mince pies.'* he smiled at his attackers, surely they would stop the beating now? The crowd of Crofters fell silent for a moment.

"What did he say?" shouted one, quickly followed by several more, lemming-like utterances. They had misheard his pointless mumblings.

'He said he's a spy!' one of them shouted. The angry, drunken, stupid mob roared back to life and collectively decided to hang poor Albert from the nearest gibbet. Albert's pitiful pleas to the crowd of *"Nein, nein!"* were either misunderstood or ignored – they did, however hang him nine times from the same gibbet, either to ensure certainty of death or perhaps they thought that was what he had been asking for."

"So it was done, Albert Himmler, dead at just twenty three years old; killed because of the Crofters' ignorance and his poor understanding of the English language, though his grandmother must also shoulder some of the blame. A contributory fact also was that no self-respecting Crofter would ever entertain the thought of eating a mince pie."

"Our friend Mr O'nad witnessed this barbaric spectacle and decided to make himself scarce. He ran along the beach, but tripped over the ship's log. Luckily he didn't hurt himself too much on the sea-sodden branch and came to rest near a book."

Heinny again took a few deep breaths and shifted his position, the pain from the recent 'procedure' on his genitals clearly etched on his face as well as his sac.

"Julia?" he asked.

"Hmm?" she responded drowsily.

"Could I trouble you for a paracetamol?"

"Of course you can." she reached into her bag, which was conveniently right next to her chair, rummaged in it for an eternity, eventually pulling out a battered box of the pain relieving medicine; popping two tablets from the foil she handed them to Heinny with a glass of water which she had also taken from her bag – the two males in the room stared at each other, perplexed.

Heinny thanked her and continued with his tale whilst gently rubbing the now swelling and bruised remnants of his scrotum. Julia found her eyes drawn to his groin momentarily, quickly snapping out of it and returning her concentration to the monkey's other tale. Heinny winked at her as he continued.

"Where were we? Ah, yes, the book. 'Kapitän-Zeitschrift' was etched in gold leaf on the leather bound cover. Luckily (for Mr O'nad, and this story) our hero had studied German prior to his arrival in England, thinking it would stand him in good stead with your Royal Family, and so he was able to read not only the cover, but also its content. Inside the cover, handwritten in ink, were the words:

"Das ist die Zeitschrift des Kapitäns Alberts Himmler des Schiffs "Dame-Glück" Hamburgs.

Der Finder dieser Zeitschrift muss heilig halten alles innerhalb für seinen Inhalt kann großes Glück und Macht verursachen.!"

"Which he quickly translated as:

"This is the Journal of Captain Albert Himmler of the ship 'Lady Luck' of Hamburg.

The finder of this journal must hold sacred everything within for its content can bring about great fortune and power."

"O'nad quickly scanned the first entry in the journal, which translated as:

> *Saturday 23rd August 1794*
> *"If you are reading this, then you have found a sacred book. You must learn from it and treasure it, for it will bring you untold power and success in life and beyond. As the reader you must also know that I am dead, and if it is at all possible, you must recover my body for it contains the source of the power and success of which I write. Without my body this journal is useless.*
> *A good day. Weather was warm and sunny, though it clouded over a little by teatime."*

"O'nad did, indeed, treasure the book, in fact he worshipped it, based his faith and future on it and eventually became 'der Halter des Geheimnisses', or 'the holder of the secret.' and enjoyed all that came with it; great power, strength and, as you will soon discover, the secret of eternal life, all of which he used to do great good in the world, but in building this goodness, O'nad made many enemies, those who would do anything to steal his power and turn it to their own evil, twisted desires. He also, as the journal requested, recovered the body of my forefather, Albert, though he didn't keep all of him. The part he needed to attain his power was Albert's scrotal sac."

Heinny sat back in his chair and sighed loudly. "I'm sorry to place such a burden upon your young shoulders, but it will soon become your responsibility to save the world from an evil foe and you must listen carefully to me so that you do not go wrong; mankind, baboon-kind will depend on your ultimate success. "

## Chapter Three

### *"A Monkeys Tale"*

Both David and Julia looked on aghast, their faces bearing a resemblance to those who suffer from catatonia[3]. Not because they had been utterly bored by the Baboon's disclosure of O'nad, but because they were totally immersed in this fabulous story.

David was the first to rouse himself (that's <u>rouse</u> and not, I repeat not, <u>arouse</u> himself).

"Amazing, absolutely amazing" he exclaimed.

"But tell me something Heinny".

"What?" responded the animal.

"All that you have divulged serves only to tell us what and who this O'nad is!"

"This is true" replied Heinny.

"Well, from what you tell us he appears to be the consummate hero and all round good guy" said David.

"That's right" added Julia. "What it doesn't explain is how you came to be here with the most horrific genital injuries I have ever come across". (Quite how many genital injuries Julia had experienced or indeed come across, either first or second hand in her time, can only be surmised!).

"You are quite right Julia." Heinny replied. "It is no accident that I found my way to your home tonight, you good people are a prophesised part of destiny. The reasons I sought you out will become apparent shortly. However, just as each story has its hero then so it has its villain."

---

[3] A baboon is actually a monkey, not an ape. Top marks to the clever people who spotted this. Don't tell the stupid or gullible people.

"Does such a villain exist in your story then?" added David.

"Indeed it does." said Heinny. "In fact it has lots of villains, but one stands out above all for his evilness shines out like a beacon from his vile, corpulent body, his name is B'stard".

"I beg your pardon!" said Julia "We'll have no filth uttered in this house." she went on to add. (The 'filth' she was referring to was of course that which is uttered verbally rather than that which is expelled bodily i.e. faecal matter. The latter of which is apparently acceptable. You will remember that Heinny lost total control of his bowels in Chapter One whilst the Snaiths looked on without comment or revulsion).

"I'm sorry if his name offends but it is his real name, the name he was Christened with, not that there are any vestiges of Christianity in him." said Heinny. "You see, he's a B'stard by name and a bastard by nature!" he angrily added.

"I won't tell you again." warned Julia.

"Apologies Julia" Heinny humbly replied. "I admit my second reference to the 'b' word was an unfortunate profanity but you must understand exactly how I feel about this person, nay, thing!" Julia accepted Heinny's apology, if only to allow him to further advance his story, now that it's getting more and more exciting.

"Please, go on." she urged.

"His name is B'stard, Mr D.T B'stard" said Heinny.

"D.T?" said David. "What do the initials stand for?"

"The 'D' stands for Dirty, quite a fitting title as you will soon begin to understand." replied Heinny.

"What about the 'T'?" asked Julia.

"The 'T' stands for Terrence, though I'm informed his close friends call him Terry or Tel." replied Heinny. "Mr Dirty B'stard, as I shall now continue to refer to him, is the villain of this tale. A villain so vile as to perhaps warrant the addition of another initial in his name." said Heinny in a rather mysterious way.

"What might that be then?" asked Julia inquisitively.

"The addition of a 'U'..... A 'U' for Utter." replied Heinny contemptuously.

"You mean Mr Dirty, Terrence, Utter B'stard?" responded Julia.

"Well yes, I suppose so." responded Heinny. "But perhaps we need not make reference to Terrence otherwise it detracts from the sinister side of his nature".

"Mr Utter Dirty B'stard it is then." added David. "So tell me... what makes him such an utter dirty B'stard?" he went on to add.

"Well, if you two can just stop bloody interrupting for a second, I'll tell you!" snapped the Baboon.

"Sorry" the pair sheepishly replied. The Snaiths looked at each other, accepted that they were perhaps being a little pedantic, if not anal, and urged their simian friend to continue.

"Mr Dirty B'stard, a man..."

"Mr Utter Dirty B'stard." interjected Julia,

"Yes." replied Heinny, "Mr Utter Dirty B'stard, a man of the most heinous nature, belongs to a secret religious sect known as The Order of the Scrotum. This order has been in existence for almost two hundred years, indeed ever since O'nad discovered the secrets of Albert Himmler's journal and began to gain the power it offered. The Order's sole purpose is to steal O'nads power and turn it to their own evil in order to dominate mankind, the world as we know it and the universe beyond; if you like, the order of the day for the Order of the Scrotum is to turn order into disorder and B'stard dishes out the orders for the Order in order that they achieve said state of disorder. Anyway, I digress; there are some pretty influential members of this order, men rich enough to fund their evil activities and assist in their search for the beloved ball bag, men who will stop at nothing to attain the power, strength and wealth it can bring. Until recently the order was governed by a monster called Colin-the-not-so-nice. Colin amounted to little as he lacked the drive and determination of his forefathers and

A Crofter's Tale (The REAL Story of The Hartlepool Monkey)

predecessors who, like our present villain, were all bastards (quite literally by name) with the exception of the creator of this order and the instigator of its evil doctrine. This person was absolutely abhorrent, evil incarnate, a man whose wickedness to man and the world knew no bounds. His name was Tobias Wat – Twat for short. Believe me when I say that never was there a more befitting name for a man who displayed so much that was so bad. With the deposing of Colin-the-not-so-nice came a new leader, a leader who's style was akin to that of the order's originator. Some would even say, and I myself would concur, that Colin's successor was and is in fact even more evil than Twat himself. This person is none other than Mr Dirty B'stard."

"Mr Utter Dirty B'stard" said Julia.

"Yes Julia." Heinny sighed.

Both David and Julia listened on incredulously, scarcely believing what they were hearing. They both gazed upon Heinny and simultaneously, at the same time, and in a synchronised fashion, together, in unison urged their friend to continue. Heinny then went on to explain further.

"Have you ever come across a book called The Monkey's Paw?"

David and Julia both responded in the negative. Heinny explained the premise of the book to the on looking Snaiths.

"The Monkey's Paw is a short story by W.W Jacobs, written in 1902. The story is based on traditional stories in which three wishes are granted. In the story the paw of a dead monkey is a talisman that grants its possessor three wishes, but the three wishes come with an enormous price." explained Heinny. "Without going too deep into Mr Jacobs' tale let me draw some of the comparisons".

"I am a simian, an ape, an anthropoid..... if you prefer, a monkey!! I come from a rather unique troop of Baboon's whose home is in the North Western industrial regions of Germany. Our uniqueness is also our curse! For you see it is not our paws that hold mystical or magic qualities, like those in Jacobs tale. Rather, these qualities can only be found in our genitalia or, more specifically, our scrotal sacs!"

"However, just like Jacobs' tale, our scrotal sacs, should they fall into the wrong hands, will grant their possessor untold power. The power to which I refer is a power strong enough for the 'owner' to take control of mankind, the world and the universe"

"Mr Dirty B'stard and his evil order know this and they have hunted me and my kind for almost a decade. Until now we have been able to evade detection and indeed capture. We have devised countless ingenious methods to avoid the attentions of our foe. Granted, most of these have involved the males tucking their scrotal sacs between their legs and donning women's clothing, a personal favourite method of mine."

"This very night however, whilst relieving myself after a few sherbets down at the Red Lion pub, I dropped my guard and indeed my sac. Unbeknown to me I was in the presence of a Dirty B'stard whose personal mission is to scour every urinal in the world in his quest for the sacred sac. Before I could finish my micturation, or indeed shake the last vestiges of simian urea from my glans, I was overcome by another slashing sensation. However, this time the slashing was not to do with the evacuation of waste liquid from my bladder. Rather, this slashing was the rending of my scrotal sac at the hands of my most feared foe."

"Before I knew it my sac and my foe were no more. I managed to hold onto what I could and that something was my left testicle, the importance of which I will now divulge. For although Mr Dirty B'stard has been given the sac, (apologies for the unnecessary pun there), he has dropped a bollock (apologies for that one too); the sac will give him what he desires, and we all know what that will be, but all is not lost just yet. For you see the teste, having such an affinity with its partner (the sac) will act as a magnet, a compass, drawing whoever holds the magical orb to its symbiotic other-half. However the orienteering capability only applies to the left testicle, the right testicle is simply, and fundamentally a regular baboons testicle. We hold 'der linke hode! Mr Dirty B'stard must be stopped before he wreaks havoc upon this world. The teste will take he who is brave enough, to the sac and indeed the enemy"

The Snaiths once again looked on aghast but this time their aghast turned to flabber and all at once they were flabbergasted.

"Who will go, will it be you Heinny?" asked David

"Alas, no," replied their friend. "It must be another".

"Who?" asked Julia with bated breath. Bated being infinitely more preferable to her usual breath as Julia suffers terribly from halitosis.

The reply from Heinny was short (about 6 inches) and straight to the point.

"You will have to go for it is written and prophesised in the Baboon scriptures that order and salvation to the sacred sac will be brought by those bearing the names "David and Julia Smith" therefore it is your destiny, and this is why it is no accident that I found my way here tonight."

"But our name is Snaith, not Smith! So it cannot be us to whom your scriptures refer or prophesise." piped David.

"Did I say Smith? What I meant to say was Snaith......" retorted Heinny in an extremely apologetic and less than convincing way. "But fear not Smi... Erm, Snaiths for you will not go alone. There is one other. That other is O'nad".

"Aw yeh O'nad... I forgot about him" said Julia. "Where does he fit in again?"

"O'nad is our greatest and bravest ally." continued Heinny. "He also knows of the danger and threat of the Order of the Scrotum and has vowed to come to our aid should one of our kind become bereft of their gooly case." he went on. "This time has come. O'nad must now be summoned. Only then can the quest to restore order be undertaken."

"How do we get in touch with O'nad then?" asked the Smiths, I mean Snaiths.

"This is where the magic starts!" announced Heinny. "In order to make him appear in person you must call his name". He went on; "Thou shalt call his name (O'nad) three times. No more, no less. Three shalt be the number of times thou callest out and the number of the calling shalt be three. Four times shalt thou not call out, nor either shalt thou call out twice, excepting that thou then proceed to three, being the third time of calling. Five is right out. Once the calling out thrice, being the third time of calling be reached then shalt thou wait. He will then appear"[4]

David and Julia dutifully complied with the simian's instructions and proceeded then to call out his name (three times – see above). Once they had done so a silence fell upon the room. The Snaiths both looked at Heinny and Heinny looked back.

"My time here is done, I must now leave!" said Heinny.

The Snaiths, confused now by what their friend had said, sought to seek some form of explanation from each other and gazed momentarily into each other's eyes. After just a few passing seconds they turned to Heinny to ask "What next?" But this was too late. He was gone. All that remained was his testicle; the magnetic, magical, scrotal, orienteering aid.

Julia picked up the bruised plum and held it close to her cheek as if to feel the last remaining remnants of the Baboon's warmth in her hands and on her face. Julia had been very much touched (not in a mental way but in an emotional way) by the events which had unfolded during the night and she now longed for Heinny to be back in the room. An overwhelming passion swept through her body, a passion which quickly turned to grief at the absence of this passing stranger in the night. She longed to

---

[4] The authors acknowledge the thrice calling text to be taken from Monty Python's Holy Grail. We have tried to obtain relevant permissions, though Graham Chapman appears not to be responding to emails.

comfort Heinny, to hold him in her arms, to caress him. She looked at the love egg and drew it close to her lips as if to suggest she was going to kiss it. This is exactly what she had in mind. She was obviously touched (this time in the mental way). No sooner had she planted her gums round the plum than her actions were abruptly halted.

"Well?" said David, apparently agitated.

"Well what?" responded Julia, confused;

"I said what did you think of his tale?"

Without thinking too hard, and whilst still holding the blood soaked testicle, Julia instantly responded "Ooh, it was lovely."

"Eh?" said David, but before she could reply a voice boomed out from the darkened corner of the room.

"I believe that belongs to me!"

The Snaiths both looked around to establish where the voice was coming from. "Could it be Heinny?" thought Julia, hopefully. It wasn't Heinny though. As the Snaiths scanned the room once more they set their gaze upon the one and only..........O'nad.

# Chapter 4

## *"Gerard's Cross"*

O'nad stood in the corner of the room; the same corner previously occupied by Heinny when David had first seen the pitiful baboon; the same corner where its bowels had given way.

"You must be O'nad?" said Julia questioningly.

# A Crofter's Tale (The REAL Story of The Hartlepool Monkey)

"Nah, it's flaming Groucho Marx; of course it's O'nad you imbecile!" retorted David, sarcastic as ever. Julia kicked his shins and stamped hard on his bare foot, David winced in agony.

"Please come forward Mr O'nad." said Julia and then both she and David quickly realised that if O'nad did as requested, he would sl...

"Holy fek!"

Their realisation had come too late as O'nad landed with a heavy thud on top of the monkeys mess.

"Oh for fek's sake!" moaned O'nad, "I can certainly see you've had a baboon here, they're always doing this, the filthy buggers." he paused, wiping his dirtied shoe across a clean area of carpet; David tutted loudly.

"I'm hoping that you are the Smiths?" he questioned.

"Snaiths!" replied Julia and David in unison.

"Snaiths?.....oh, ah, erm yes, Snaiths, that's it."

"Please Mr O'nad come forward so we can see you and help you get cleaned up; I'm so sorry about this." apologised Julia. O'nad stood shakily and for a fleeting moment David saw Groucho Marx. It was only fleeting – the same black-rimmed spectacles and moustache surrounding an enormous nose, the wild hair and that trademark cigar held just above the top lip, no doubt about it, it was Groucho Marx – and then it was gone and a very different character stood before them.

Gerard O'nad  - (Authors note: descriptive - Short in many ways, short tempered, short in height and severely short sighted, short trousers…though not short of a bob-or-two./ despite purporting to have come from Ireland - speaks with broad Glaswegian accent...)

"You do realise the implications of your calling me, I presume?, our mutual friend Mr Himmler will have fully explained it to you both?" he asked;

"We think we get the general gist, though we don't understand why it had to be us." replied Julia

"For it is written!" responded O'nad haughtily; David flinched. "It has long been prophesised that a young couple by the name of," he paused again "sorry, what was your name again?"

*"Snaith"* they both replied, eyes rolling skywards as they did so.

"Of course. Yes, it has long been prophesised that a young couple, by the name of Snaith, will assist me in my fight for the freedom from persecution of the plum pouch, or as my friend Heinny put it – 'gooly case', so it is prophesised; so shall it be; and tonight, my friends, our fight is almost at an end"

David and Julia looked at one another, eyebrows raised.

"So, what now? How do we find this evil Dirty B'stard and, more to the point, what do we have to do when, if, we find him?" said David.

"We, you, simply have to retrieve the gooly case, reunite it with its testicle and return it to its rightful owner." responded O'nad.

"Simply? just how simple is 'simply'?" asked David.

"Ah, well, that's the difficult part." replied O'nad confusingly. "Firstly, I must take you to the place where it all began. The little fishing village in the North-East where I landed when I first left Ireland, and the place where I came by my vast powers; the place which strikes fear into the heart of all anthropoids."

"Where, where?" piped Julia.

"A place so barren and desolate that only the hardy go there and only those with the strongest stomachs can stay, a place where greed and depravity reign supreme over the goodness of this land, a place where…"

"Oh for goodness sake, just tell us will you?" piped David this time, becoming impatient.

"Hartlepool." responded O'nad, almost apologetically. Once more, in unison and together, as one voice, the Snaiths said *"Of Course, Hartlepool"* in a manner that would suggest they had been a bit thick in not recognising this fact earlier, which, if we're honest, they had been.

And so the Snaiths readied themselves to set off, with Gerard O'nad, on their magical adventure to find the missing genitalia.

# Chapter 5

*"Be careful what you wish for....! (Carts and all)"*

During preparations for their journey O'nad tried to put all of the pieces of the jigsaw into place.

"No doubt Heinny told you of Tobias?" asked O'nad.

Julia began to respond with "Oh, you mean twa...."

"His name is Tobias!" O'nad cut her sentence short abruptly, angrily. The Snaiths looked upon O'nad and observed a change in his expression.

"Toby was a very, very dear friend of mine." exclaimed O'nad. By now both Julia and David were growing more curious as the events of the evening began to unfold.

"A friend?" asked Julia inquisitively.

"Yes." sighed O'nad. "Allow me to put you in the complete picture. On the day of Albert's death, at the hands of the drunken and ignorant Crofters, to which I was a witness, I met Tobias Wat, for he was also at those violent proceedings. After finding the captain's journal and securing it safely in my knapsack, as the Crofters were about to carry out their evil act of execution, I felt compelled to leave as quickly as possible for fear of my own safety and indeed my own life! I was not the only person there present to make this decision. Tobias also focussed on distancing himself from the unfolding aberration. As I ran along the beach back to the village I ran into Tobias, quite literally. We both tumbled to the ground and found ourselves entwined, one on top of the other. As we were still in close proximity to the sea a wave came lapping up to our feet and as far as our midriffs (a scene not dissimilar to that in 'From Here to Eternity' involving Burt Lancaster & Deborah Kerr). Both of us startled, and at the same time embarrassed, we quickly got to our feet brushed ourselves down and turned to each other offering a hand of apology. The ice was quickly broken and we smiled. It was the first time we had been able to do so during the unfolding events."

"We both instinctively knew that our next course of action was to get back to the village as soon as possible and from then on we accompanied each other on the way. Tobias introduced himself, as did I. We shared the same views and thoughts of what the Crofters were doing to the poor and forlorn ape. When we got back to the village Tobias invited me into his cottage to dry my clothes and to take some hot tea. I gratefully accepted."

"That doesn't sound like the Twa... I mean Tobias that Heinny referred to" responded David.

"Allow me to further explain" said O'nad. "That afternoon, in Tobias' cottage, we talked for hours. In the main company was infinitely more preferable to solitude at that time! Toby told me of himself. He explained that he was a humble pie maker, one that specialised in the 'mince' variety. He went on to explain that he had put all of his savings into building a business which he hoped would sustain him and his family throughout their remaining lives. Alas, the Crofters did not share nor appreciate the culinary delights of Tobias's sweet mince comestibles. Consequently his business failed and, through sheer poverty, he had lost his wife and eight children to starvation. In retrospect, and between me and you, I believe that broader business diversity could have saved his plight, that and the occasional abstention from marital conjugal activities.

# A Crofter's Tale (The REAL Story of The Hartlepool Monkey)

I mean, who really needs to have eight kids!!!! Anyway I digress. What I could see was that Tobias, Toby, was a broken man simply trying to survive in the harsh and brutal world of late eighteenth century England. After all it wasn't Toby's' fault that the Crofters didn't like mince pies."

"I took pity on Toby and from that point on we became good friends. I also became his most loyal (and only) customer at Ye Olde Pie Shoppe. So now you will see why I prefer to call him Tobias or Toby, rather than the name given to you by Heinny"

"So why is he now so feared as Heinny explained to us?" asked the Snaiths.

"In order to explain that I need to first tell you what happened to me once I had escaped the scene of Albert's murder with Albert's book tucked away in my bag…..!

"Once I had returned home from Toby's that evening I readied myself for bed, got beneath the sheets and closed my eyes as tightly as I could. I did this to quicken sleep, so as to fall into a dream that would take me away from the nightmares of the day. Sleep, however, evaded me and I found myself tossing (a motion of restlessness rather than an act of onenism) and turning. The events of the day tormented me and were being replayed continuously in my mind's eye. Then I remembered the book. It was still in my bag. Curiosity took hold and I reached for the bag which hung at my bedstead. I opened the book and proceeded to scan the pages. The book told the story of Albert and his kind. Albert, as Heinny will no doubt have told you, came from a unique Flange (Yes, Flange as this is the official, collective noun for a group of Baboons and not the author being lewd again). The Flange was, and still is, blessed with unique mystical powers, or rather their scrotums are. You see every $7^{th}$ generation of these Baboons a miracle happens, for every male member of the flange is endowed with magical genitalia; Albert was $7^{th}$ generation and his 'gooly case' possessed the key to unlocking the powers which were useless to him, but which could ultimately benefit mankind.

However, should just one member lose his magical sac, then the power is taken from the entire flange and transferred to whosoever takes or finds it. Albert documented clearly what the finder of the book needed to do in order to benefit from the force held within and I was impelled to carry out his instructions. This, however, meant that I would need to return to the scene of the atrocity. I hurried myself from my warm and safe bed, donned my clothes and set forth back to the site of the hanging. It was well past midnight and all was quiet and still. I stealthily approached the hangman's gibbet, which was macabrely displaying its pitiful trophy, Albert! I stopped, took a pause, in respect for this poor creature, then under the light of the moon read from the pages of his journal to decipher what I needed to do next. The answer came quickly as I hurriedly read the text. It simply said *"Remove the scrotum and all will be yours."* I did as the instruction asked and hacked away at the deceased simian's leather wallet until it dropped softly into my waiting palms. Once I had carried out this task I made haste back to my abode to read carefully what the next steps would be."

"Back at my home I sat at the table, book in one hand and scrotum in the other. This was not an uncommon way for me to spend my nights at the time, though I would usually be flicking through the pages of an 'art pamphlet' rather than a captains journal, nor would it have been a baboons scrotum I held in my hand. I read on. All I needed to do now, according to the text, was to make my three wishes using the incantations within the book. These incantations were already written and it fell upon the reader to recite them word for word, with no deviation from the text, as they appeared in the book. Any deviation would not lose the wisher their wish, but what they wished for would either not happen, or happen in the manner of their corrupted incantation.

The book explained that three wishes would be granted to whoever holds the 7th generation testicle hammock but gave a warning asking the holder to be careful what they wish for…and not deviate from the text. At first I dismissed the book and the promise of three wishes as pure fantasy, believing instead that they were the ramblings of an idiot. But then I recalled what I had witnessed that very day. A talking ape, captaining a sea vessel, brutally murdered (blame his grandmother for this) and an extremely curious book. Perhaps there might be something in this after all I thought, besides what did I have to lose, apart from my own sanity? At this point I decided that I would make my three wishes"

The Snaith's by this point had been extremely quiet, totally immersed in O'nad's tale, when Julia piped up;

"What did you wish for, what did you wish for....?"

O'nad obliged and began to relay back to the Snaiths that which he had asked.

"The first of my wishes was, as most people in my situation would make, to be wealthy beyond my wildest dreams. To have and to hold more wealth than any mortal can imagine or dare to dream. I found the relevant incantation and began to read aloud. Once I had asked this wish, holding scrotum in hand (Albert's that is, and not my own) I was overcome by a sense of excitement, an excitement that drove every last molecule of moisture from my mouth. I reached for my cup and drank the contents empty but this failed to satiate my thirst. I got up from my chair to fetch the water jug from the kitchen dresser. However, as I rose I heard a curious sound. The sound was that of metal hitting a stone surface. The sound repeated itself and grew more intense as I approached the dresser. Looking down towards the floor I could see small, round objects glinting on the surface of my stone floor. I got down on my knees to examine, more closely, what these objects could be. They were coins, gold coins. Where were they coming from? They were coming from my pockets. There were 50 coins, then 100, then 200 and so on. I put my hand inside my pocket and the cascade of coins ceased. Is this all the wealth I get I thought? I took my hand from the pocket once more and the cascade resumed. In, out, in, out I went with my pocket and soon realised that this action served to 'turn' the money on and off alternately. My wish had come true I was rich, extremely rich."

"Fascinating quite fascinating" said David. "That's your first wish. What of your remaining wishes?"

"Yes!" joined Julia. "What did you wish for next?"

"My next wish went as follows" replied O'nad. "Given my good fortune (quite literally) I realised that I would spend the rest of my living days in the lap of luxury, but for how long would that be? I was already halfway through my three score years and ten, yet life expectancy during the eighteenth century dictated that many a person would suffer an early demise, what with poor sanitation and wide-spread disease."

"And thick Crofters!" interjected David, smiling to himself. O'nad continued, "How long would I benefit from my abundance of wealth? I pondered for a moment and then it came to me. I could have my wealth for as long as I desired, or indeed wished! Flicking through the pages of the journal again, quite by chance, I unexpectedly came upon the correct incantation. Wiping the page clean and holding scrotum firmly in my grasp, I uttered my second wish, reading the incantation word for word, I wished for eternal life. I would live forever, forever being rich. Having spoken my wish I was overcome with a new sensation. This sensation ran the length and breadth of my body and from the inside to the outside and back again. I walked around the room and suddenly realised that the inherent pain in my lower limbs, borne out of a bout of scurvy a few years previous, had gone, replaced with an overwhelming sense of vitality, vim, verve and vigour (and any other adjectives beginning with the letter 'v' one could conceive). Could it be? I thought to myself; am I immortal? Will I live forever? Time would surely tell and my existence here today, some 200 years later serves testament to this"

"You lucky swine" exclaimed David "Any chance you could help us out with our mortgage repayments seeing as though we are doing you a favour in this quest of yours/ours?"

"You can have whatever you desire, if money is your desire, once we have completed our quest" said O'nad.

"Oooh, that's lovely" said Julia. "And can we have a new dish-washer as well?" She added.

"Why I oughta......!" David remonstrated. Julia realised she was being rather silly making such a request and sought to redeem herself by asking what O'nad's third and last wish had been.

"My third and last wish was a difficult one to make" said O'nad. "I pondered to myself for what seemed like an eternity. I was rich beyond my dreams; I could live forever to take advantage of this. What more could I want or need? In a moment of hastiness I made my third and final wish. I remembered how I coveted my neighbour during the summer past when he acquired a brand new cart. I admired this cart greatly and dreamt that one day I might have one I could call my own. I could, if I had taken a moment to think a bit more considerately, have been able to afford any cart that I wanted, for I now had the means. Alas, my impetuosity and envy for my neighbours cart had swept over me and the wish was made. Luckily there was such an incantation in the book and so I wished for a brand new cart"

"You wished for a cart......!!!!!" said David in a rather condescending way. But then again David, as we know is rather expert in this mode of behaviour as Julia is able to testify.

"Ah, but it was no ordinary cart that I wished for." smirked O'nad.

"Really?" said Julia. "See, it was no ordinary cart David." she retorted in a reasonably condescending way. (Julia was getting better at being condescending and sarcastic for she had a good mentor in her husband).

"What was so special about this cart then" asked David.

"Well" replied O'nad. "Carts in the late eighteenth century were basic by design and the best one could hope for in terms of speed of travel was around 4mph, irrespective of the quality of nag pulling the vehicle. Rather, what I wished for was a cart that was twice as fast, one that could easily get into double figures making my cart the 'Ferrari' equivalent in its day"

"So, let me get this right" said David (condescending tone, yet again).
"You are fabulously rich, you will live forever and you have a cart that can reach the break neck speed of 10mph?"

"Yes, but that's not all." defended O'nad. "For you see I can summon this cart to my presence wherever and whenever I like, for it is a magic cart"

"Oh, I do apologise. The bit about the summoning makes all the difference I'm sure." said David, that's right, sarcastically.

"Ignore him Mr O'nad" said Julia. "He's always like this, why I married him God only knows. Given that you'd made your three wishes what then?"

"Unable to sleep for the rest of the night due to the unbelievable nature of what had just happened to me I sat and absorbed the intensely good feelings that were surging through my body at the time. Before too long, dawn arrived. Dawn was the girl from next door who I was seeing on a casual basis, and we spent the remnants of the night together indulging ourselves in a series of intimate activities which required the use of my own scrotum rather than that of the simian Albert. At the crack of dawn I broke wind, and dawn (and Dawn) was no more; replaced instead with bright rays of sunshine streaking through the gaps in my curtains. It was a new day, the start of the rest of my life; I wanted to celebrate and to start my celebrations I needed to tell someone of my good fortune, but who would believe such a fantastical tale?"

I visited Toby shortly after 07:00. He was still in bed so I attempted to wake him with a furious banging. As luck would have it he 'swung that way' so he was extremely accommodating but never-the-less asked that if I needed to wake him in the future could I knock on the door like others. I apologised and agreed to do as he'd asked".

"Is the homosexual nature of this tale absolutely necessary?" asked David whilst simultaneously retching.

"I suppose not" said O'nad. "But now you understand the connection between the two of us, how close we were." he went on to explain.

"If you were **that** close" said Julia. "What happened between the two of you that has lead to you being so at odds?"

"One word and one word only. He was greedy." sighed O'nad.

"That's three words isn't it? What do you mean?" asked David.

"At first, Toby and I got on really well. I helped him with his pie shop business and got him out of debt for the first time in his life. Sure, he knew the full details of what had happened to me on that fateful night as I shared every detail with him, even down to the secrets secreted within Albert's journal, to which he had access always. However, over a period of time, and for reasons I need not go into at this juncture, I sensed deterioration in our relationship and we began to drift further apart. I first suspected something to be dramatically wrong when I happened upon him copying, by hand, the contents of Albert's journal. When I confronted him about this he simply said he was making a duplicate in case the original was lost and, being a trusting soul and deeply fond of Toby, I agreed that the book needed to be safeguarded. Little did I know that he was, in fact, plotting to benefit from the powers of the journal himself, for he had become consumed by envy in much the same way I had with my neighbour's cart.

One night, whilst Toby was out, I let myself into his shop and examined the book which he was replicating from Albert's original. Inside the perfect replica journal were a number of loose leaf inserts. Many of these inserts were new pie recipes he had been intent on trying, one of which was for a snack called a 'Cornish Pasty' whilst another was for a 'Sausage Roll'. I vaguely recall him speaking to me of these ideas but he was put off pursuing their development as he was convinced the idea or appeal would not catch on. Anyway, just as I was about to put the replica journal and its loose leaf inserts back I happened across another insert. This insert had been inserted between the other inserts in a way which would suggest that the insert in question was inserted with the sole intention of being mistaken for any ordinary insert. However, this insert was different as it did not contain recipe ideas for savoury comestibles. Instead it read a more sinister tone."

"What was it, what did it say?" said Julia.

"It was entitled *"The Order of the Scrotum"* and described Tobias' devious intent. Tobias had described how, although he could not benefit personally from the powers of the scrotum during his lifetime he would make sure he could at a later time. Tobias set forth plans to create this Order and to pass the key to its riches from generation to generation. He had done this knowing the next scrotal windfall would not be for another seven generations of Albert's Flange. He had correctly calculated this to be in the first decade of the twenty first century, now! He also knew that passing this secret on carried great risks. What if the person within the Order at the time of the seventh generation advent refused, as Tobias had laid out in his Order's doctrine, to use one of the wishes to resurrect him? Tobias had thought carefully of this and simply laid the bait which would appeal to anyone's greedy and envious nature. He falsely described in his copy of the journal that the person who obtains the next seventh generation scrotum will have limitless wishes, not just three, but only on the understanding that they resurrect the founder of the Order. Tobias knew this ploy would not fail as there would be no perceived losers in this, and he would ultimately get his own way and benefit as I do, and have done all this time. I questioned Tobias indirectly over the copying of the book the next day to see what kind of reaction I would get. He continued to defend his actions in the way he always had by referring to the copy as a 'safeguard'. By now I knew that Toby had changed. He had become devious, shallow and greedy. His longing for what I had produced great conflict in him and he became a different person to the one I had met just a few years earlier. The day following my indirect challenge to him he disappeared, and I never saw him again." an intense sadness washed over O'nad as he continued. "Toby vanished, as did his journal and his foundations for the Order of the Scrotum along with the bright yellow necktie I'd bought him for his birthday. All that remained were the prototype recipes for the 'Cornish Pasty' and 'Sausage Roll' which in later years I developed to be universal best sellers in the field of savoury convenience foods."

"During the last decade I have tracked down the Order of the Scrotum and its present leader, the infamous Mr D T B'stard. I have monitored their activities as well as monitoring the arrival of the 7$^{th}$ generation Flange. Over the past years, months, weeks, days, hours and indeed minutes, the paths of all parties have drawn closer until the inevitable critical collision. The collision I speak of was the rending of Heinny's scrotum at the hands of Mr D T B'stard this very night. Therefore, we are in haste for the chase is now on to track the sac down and to do what we can to prevent Mr D T B'stard's intentions to resurrect the body and soul of Tobias Wat"

## Chapter 6
### *"Make Haste for Hartlepool"*

As soon as O'nad had completed his epic tale they began their journey.

Once outside the spring warmth seemed to have been washed away by the earlier violent storm; Julia instinctively huddled into her coat. Luckily, the storm had abated and all that remained was a light drizzle and a cool breeze.

O'nad led the way to his vehicle. At the kerbside sat a gleaming Mercedes Benz, jet black with the biggest alloy wheels David had ever seen.

"Is this what we're travelling in?" asked David tentatively; Julia recognised the concern in her husbands voice.

"Oh David, it'll be fine." she attempted to soothe.

"Is there a problem Mr Smi... Snaith?" asked O'nad, his urgency barely concealed.

"No, it'll be fi.." began Julia, finding her sentence severed by the acid tongue of her new husband.

"No!, No it won't be fine, Julia. It's alright for you; you don't have what I have. Please, Mr O'nad is there any other way of getting to Hartlepool?" he asked, the pleading tone of his voice undisguised.

"Don't you like my car?" asked O'nad; "We must make haste, this will get us there in no time."

"Your car is beautiful." responded David, "It's just that..., well, it's just that I er...";

"David's scared of cars." tutted Julia, showing little regard for her partners' phobia, and sounding almost child-like in her condescension.

# A Crofter's Tale (The REAL Story of The Hartlepool Monkey)

"We don't have time for this! We have to get to Hartlepool before Mr Dirty B'stard uncovers the truth about Tobias's false prophesy. How else did you think we could get there?" asked O'nad, not at all concerned about David's fears, and ever so slightly hacked off that Heinny had stumbled across such a pair of idiots at such a critical time in history. "Come along now, and let's have none of this silliness!" he scolded.

"Bu.." began David. "Bu.. bleuuurrggh..!!
The projectile vomit which exploded from David's gullet was sufficient to halt O'nad's anger momentarily.

"Bleuurrrrrggh……..heuuurrgh; I……c..raaallllpph….can't do….heurrrgh…it!!!"
Julia had never seen her husband like this and instantly felt a wave of guilt wash over her as she thought back to the poo-based biscuit she had fed him earlier, could this have been the cause of such a violent stomach upset?

"What the bloody hell are we going to do now?" shouted O'nad, his anger returning; "I've waited two hundred fekking years for this night and I'm damned sure I'm not going to let some vomiting freak ruin it all now, can't you give him something to calm him down?" he pleaded with Julia;

"Hit him!" she replied;

"Wh..heurrrgh..what?" spluttered David,

"What?" asked O'nad;

"Hit him!" she repeated, "Knock him out, then he won't know he's in the car!"

"Noooo!" shouted David "I'm allergic to all things automotive (except, perhaps, the Robin Reliant) if I so much as go within an inch of the car, my throat will swell up and suffocate me; I will almost certainly die, surely you know this Julia?" Julia looked to the floor, the smirk on her face ever so slightly visible through the dark night; unconvincingly she responded

"Sorry David, I forgot!"

O'nad was becoming more frustrated by the passing, potentially crucial, minutes being wasted.

"Wait! I have my third wish!" He excitedly interjected.

Without waiting for a response, he clapped his hands four times in quick succession. Instantly a blaze of bright white light filled the street; faintly a horse's whinny could be heard alongside the sound of silver shod hooves against wet tarmac. Before their eyes stood O'nad's third wish.

"You've got to be kidding?" questioned Julia.

"I assure you, young lady, I am deadly serious" replied O'nad; "Now get on, both of you. Quickly!" he shouted; David and Julia quickly hauled themselves up onto the back of the wooden cart, O'nad took the crop from the side of the cart and whipped the nag into action; Julia squealed with delight as she felt the sting from the crop. At the same time O'nad gently climbed atop his faithful old mare and gently uttered the words "Walk on" into her ear. The clip-clop of the horse's hooves seemed to resonate throughout the normally quiet south London street.

In no time; well, after some considerable time, the carriage reached its top speed as they cantered towards the end of their street. It was at this point that David spotted it; at the end of the street sat a weather beaten, forlorn looking, Robin Reliant. He shouted out to O'nad who called the horse to a halt; the trio sat for a while, pondering the pro's and cons of switching vehicles, but all of them soon came to the inevitable (correct) conclusion that the sad three-wheeler would probably expire before they got out of the city; at least their current carriage had fewer things that could go wrong with it.

# Chapter 7
*"Watch out for Whippets!"*

At the precise moment that O'nad and his cart left Somers Place, London SW2, exactly two hundred and seventy miles away, in a windswept and whippet strewn side street of Hartlepool, stood the menacing figure of Mr Dirty B'stard, clutching a piece of paper, an insert of some sort, upon which, in the aged scrawl of Tobias Wat, were written the coordinates to the secret location of the book, so avidly cosseted by the Order of The Scrotum – the Captains Journal of Albert Himmler.

"I'm nearly there, my Lord and Master, soon you will live again, and we will share immeasurable riches and power." he muttered to himself. A passer by on the opposite side of the street noticed the oddly dressed B'stard and caught his eye. The icy glower he returned made the hairs on the back of her neck stand out almost painfully and she scurried away, eyes fixed on the ground ahead of her.

B'stard wore a long black leather trench coat and, perched upon the top of his balding head, the flat cap he had bought this very day in London; the salesman at the 'Northern Delights' clothing boutique in Carnaby Street had assured him that it was what all trendy northerners were wearing this season. B'stard had had no reason to doubt him at the time, but now wondered if he'd been sold a dud, as he had seen not one other soul wearing a similar item since leaving Middlesbrough. He silently, but menacingly, swore to rip out the salesman's eyes upon his return to London.

According to his GPS navigation device, he was but two hundred feet from the prize he had sought for so long. He reached into one of his coat's many pockets to ensure that he still had the

# A Crofter's Tale (The REAL Story of The Hartlepool Monkey)

magical furry sac which would help him summon his Master. It was there, still slick with the baboons blood and, of course, still housing a solitary testicle. It concerned him that he had not succeeded in securing both of the creatures' love eggs; for although he knew the significance of the symbiosis between sac and testicles, he could not be sure which testicle he had in his possession. If he held the left testicle he would have the right one, however if it was the right one he had he would have the wrong one; the only question left unanswered was, was it right or wrong? He countered his concerns with the thought that the baboon had probably bled to death by now and smiled to himself. Time was on his side.

He turned the corner, as instructed by the satellite system, and found, to his dismay, that a gleaming new supermarket had been erected and now stood directly on the site of the hidden book, the site of the hanging two hundred years ago, of Albert Himmler. Not overly perturbed by the new construction he proceeded to walk to the exact spot in the store beneath which laid his quarry. Purely coincidentally this was right next to the Meat and Savoury Pastries counter which was laden with products from the immensely popular 'O'nad's Sweet 'n' Savouries' range; to his all-consuming glee, he found himself standing upon a hatch of some sort; obviously put in to allow access to services or utility cables, but quite handy as it would mean he wouldn't have to drill through the stone floor to bring him closer to the book.

Reaching into the deepest pocket of his coat his fingers came upon the shaft of his sword, the tool he would use to lift the hatch and hack at the ground beneath; he gripped the shaft, intending to whip out the deadly tool and begin his onerous task but, upon glancing around him, he noticed that the store was still quite busy with late evening shoppers desperate for a bargain, he would surely be overcome by security guards if he was caught, next to the pork, sword in hand. He released the shaft and sighed heavily.

"It must be delayed, Master, for there is too much danger here at present." he whispered. He pushed his way through the throng of shoppers at the checkouts to make his way to the exit, deliberately kicking the shins of those unlucky enough to get in his way and ignoring their disgruntled grumblings.

As he reached the exit he noticed a sign in the window which advertised a vacancy within the bustling business –

**"Night Shift Security Guard required – no experience necessary.**
**Uniform supplied.**
**£5.25 per hour – Would suit recent graduate –**
**immediate start to right candidate!"**

it declared. B'stard instantly caught on to the plot.

Having secured the position of Night Security Guard, B'stard set about ensuring that his patrol brought him to the Meat and Savoury Pastries section of the store on a regular basis. Being the sole guard on duty at night he would have plenty of time to look for the hidden book. If he should be found below the shop floor, he would simply use the excuse that he had 'heard something down there'. The plan could not fail. He had thought of every conceivable eventuality.

Some three weeks after beginning their journey, a tired and dishevelled O'nad, Julia and David, arrived at the outskirts of Hartlepool. To Julia's obvious and extremely over the top display of delight, they were greeted at the town border by none other than Heinny.

"Welcome to Hartlepool." he said releasing himself from Julia's excited grip; Julia reluctantly let go of Heinny's hand.

"Gerard O'nad, I presume?" he questioned the cart driver, to which O'nad responded "Of course Mr Himmler, thank you for meeting us here." Heinny continued:

"Come, we have lots to do. I have uncovered the whereabouts of Mr Dirty B'stard and he is close to recovering Twat's journal and the false prophesy. If we can get to him before he raises Tobias we can try to convince him of the folly of such an action. Follow me."

## Chapter 8
### *"The Last Temptation of Granny Smith..!"*

B'stard stood below the shop floor of the gleaming supermarket, in the exact spot where a gibbet once exhibited the forlorn and bloodied carcasses of those who saw fit to upset the Crofters of Hartlepool. One such victim, certainly not the last, was Albert Himmler.

He'd been digging every night since taking up his post of night security guard three weeks ago, and had so far carved his way through the concrete floor of the store's basement and its foundations before reaching solid clay. With the constant stabbing and slashing, his sword had soon become worn and useless, and he'd replaced the tool with a pneumatic drill and spade.

Finally, at around six feet below the basement floor, he began to find evidence of what had once occupied the site, decaying wood, pottery, coins, ropes, bones and hair; all of which would indicate that he was indeed in the correct place. A geophysical survey of the ground beneath him had found evidence that a building, possibly a watch tower of wood construction, had also once stood on the site, beneath where the gibbet had been erected, probably housing ancient Britons on watch for invading Vikings. B'stard briefly thought that he should call in the Time

# A Crofter's Tale (The REAL Story of The Hartlepool Monkey)

Team crew to put in a few trenches before refocusing on the task in hand. The next thrust of his spade made contact with a solid object.

A few more hacks at the earth revealed a square shaped object wrapped in what looked like a hessian bag; he reached for the remnants of his sword and began to stab at the soil surrounding the bag. Once he had uncovered enough of the cloth to get a decent grip he began to tug the bag whilst simultaneously stabbing with his sword. A few good tugs later, still frantically stabbing with his sword, the bag came free. The rush of release was enough to momentarily unbalance B'stard and he fell, knees trembling, with a crashing thud, first to his knees and then forward into the small hole where the bag had sat, undisturbed, for over two hundred years. He let out a scream of horror as he noticed what he had just landed on.

A mud caked mask of death stared back up from the hole; the yellowish, ghoulish grin of the skull belying its sinister aura; a deep red earth worm slithered from one of the eye sockets, giving the illusion that the eye was crying tears of blood. Below the decaying bone of the bottom jaw, just poking out from the compacted soil, B'stard noticed a fragment of bright yellow cloth.

Returning his attention to the hessian sack he had just hauled from the ground, he noticed that the top of the bag had been tied with the same yellow material. It looked like some kind of necktie. B'stard quickly untied what remained of the knot and pulled open the rotting sack. His heart was pounding in his chest as if it was going to explode, he could feel the blood rushing through his veins and his breathing became erratic. Inside the bag he saw it, his prize and that of his predecessors and all followers of the Order of the Scotum, he could clearly make out the script etched into the leather bound cover and, although he could not read or speak German, he knew exactly what it said:

### *'Kapitän-Zeitschrift'*

The journal of Albert Himmler; now he had everything he needed to complete the puzzle. He reached into the trench coat

A Crofter's Tale (The REAL Story of The Hartlepool Monkey)

pocket and removed the mangled ball pouch and its accompanying testicle; holding it in his hands momentarily before laying it gently on top of the book. His goal was within reach. Soon he would enjoy the fruits of his labour, everything he could ever wish for. But first he had to refer to the slip of paper he had brought with him to see what he needed to do to summon the return of his Lord and Master, Tobias Wat.

Taking the crumpled bit of paper from his inside breast pocket he gently unfolded it and knelt beside the book he had just toiled for three long weeks to find, and once again picked up the baboons scrotal sac.

Reading from the paper, whilst cupping the baboon's ball bag, B'stard began his incantation:

*"I wish, this night, for one so fair*
*To fulfil the prophesy all can share*
*Return Tobias Wat alive to me;*
*As he once was and used to be*
*For now and all eternity"*

Silence followed; for what appeared to be an eternity, until B'stard began to think he had failed in his quest to resurrect the life of Tobias Wat, founder of the Order of the Scrotum. He listened carefully for any sign of his arrival and then, in the silence that prevailed in the darkened basement, he heard the faintest, mouse like, squeak. Looking down once more to the grisly grave beneath him he saw the hideous vision that was Tobias Wat. Well, his face at least.

Tobias spluttered and gasped as he filled his lungs with the first air he had breathed for more than two centuries. Each deep inhalation was quickly followed by equally deep exhalation and this was repeated for a few moments. Tobias then proceeded to cough and splutter some more. He coughed in a way that was reminiscent of a forty a day cigarette smoker, one who shuns the thought of 'low tar' or ultra-light' brands, preferring instead to go for the unfiltered, full tar variety (incidentally, Tobias had never smoked when he was alive which is just as well as the effects on his resurrection would no doubt have been more intense).

Tobias eventually overcame his coughing 'fit' and was able to compose his breathing more readily. B'stard sensed that the figure lying before him was becoming more alert and conscious by the second until finally he uttered, in a trembling and almost apologetic tone;

"Tobias Wat….. are you….erm… are you Tobias Wat founder of the Order of the Scrotum?"

Tobias peered up at B'stard and attempted to respond. However, the two centuries in which he had lain in his grave had taken their toll, and no matter how hard he tried, he could not muster a sound from his lips. B'stard once again asked

"Tobias?"

This time Tobias mouthed his response whilst simultaneously nodding his head as far as he could, given that it was impacted in solid clay. This was all the confirmation that B'stard needed. His quest was over and his deepest wishes now appeared all the more closer, all the more real.

B'stard, who by this time was overwhelmed with a sense of euphoria, began to remove the clay and earth from around the body of Tobias. The very clay and earth that had entombed him yet preserved him for all this time. The process was carried out with extreme care and diligence as B'stard did not want to compromise all of his hard labours up to this point. After almost twenty minutes of furious digging, B'stard was at the point where he could secure the release of Tobias. Throughout all of this time Tobias became more and more conscious. He could feel the strength return to his body and could sense all of his faculties returning, including the power of speech!

B'stard had now succeeded in removing the last vestiges of earth from the body of Tobias and, with his right arm outstretched and offered to Tobias said

"Let me help you my Lord. Take my hand and be free from this nightmare".

"Yes." responded Tobias and he too offered up his right arm in order to accept B'stards.

As they attempted to connect B'stard noticed something was not quite right. When he offered up his right hand to Tobias there was nothing in return. B'stards hand simply grasped at thin air. Thinking nothing of this he instead took hold of Tobias by his forearm and dragged him to his feet. They both stood facing one another each attempting to calibrate the other until the uncomfortable silence was broken yet again; it was Tobias who spoke first.

"I am Tobias Wat, founder of the Order of the Scrotum, and I extend my thanks to the one who has brought me back again and fulfilled my prophesy." he went on to add "Who are you?" B'stard replied

"My name is B'stard, Mr D T B'stard, your most humble and loyal servant." and in doing so offered, once again, his right hand. Tobias, in a reflex response to this act of friendship and common courtesy offered up his hand, but this is where the intended handshake ended. Tobias looked upon his own limb only to discover that his hand was missing.

"What the fu....!" he cried out. B'stard was bemused by this and immediately sensed all was not well. Tobias panicked and quickly proceeded to examine himself rather rigorously. First of all he checked that his other hand (left) was where he had left it (apologies for the unnecessary pun there) and it was.

"Thank goodness!" thought Tobias. Using his left hand he then frantically fumbled around the entire surface of his body in an attempt to check if anything else was missing. As he ran his hand over his body his breathing became erratic. He prodded and pulled at every muscle, sinew and external extremity, all the time repeating *"Oh my God, oh, my God"* Eventually, having affirmed to himself that everything else was intact he let out a huge sigh of relief and slumped forlornly to his knees.

"Oh, yes….mmm…that's a relief" he muttered.

B'stard was, by now, growing more curious as to the unfolding peculiar behaviour of his Master and asked

"What is it Master that causes you to be so distressed?"

"My hand, my hand, I've lost my hand" replied Tobias.

"Please, let me help you to your feet again my Lord." said B'stard. "I don't understand." B'stard went on to say.

"Then please, Mr B'stard, allow me the opportunity to explain." Offered Tobias.

Tobias proceeded to tell B'stard all about the Order of the Scrotum and how he had conceived his plan to be resurrected and to bring untold power to himself and all associated members of the Order. He went on to tell B'stard of his relationship (albeit slightly censored) with O'nad and how his own jealousy and envy at what O'nad had had lead him to his course of action. B'stard, of course, knew of all these plans and it was these that had brought him and his quest to the one that now stood before him. He none-the-less listened, both carefully and dutifully, if only to reaffirm that the premise of the Order was, and still is, as he expected.

"I understand all of what you have explained Master but why were you so shocked when you discovered your right hand to be missing?" asked B'stard.

"It all happened many years ago when I lived, for the first time, in the town known as Hartlepool. My first life was a miserable existence for me and times were very hard. I knew hardship extremely well and it frequented my life on numerous occasions. Whenever I encountered such hardship it was not uncommon for me to go without food for days and even weeks, as the extent of my poverty meant that I could not afford to satiate my hunger by honest means. In an instance of pure desperation I found

# A Crofter's Tale (The REAL Story of The Hartlepool Monkey)

myself to drawn to the idea of procuring nourishment by a less than honest way. At the time of my last encounter with poverty, I was living in shrubland, next to a local charitable institution for the blind. The institution in question was wholly self-sufficient and provided well for its patrons. They had a small apple orchard in their grounds which bore a veritable abundance of fruit. Whilst walking past the grounds one day, feeling the painful pangs of hunger, I espied the apples and, without thinking or having a care for the moral nature of my subsequent actions, I vaulted the perimeter fence and seized a solitary fruit which I devoured on site much to my great satisfaction".

"Your actions seem to me to be reasonable given your predicament my Lord." responded B'stard in an empathetic way.

"You would think so Mr B'stard and if it had concluded there that would have been the end of it. However, unbeknown to myself I was being observed by one of the institutes occupants (clearly this occupant was not blind, but in fact the manager) and all at once I was pounced upon, flung to the ground and for want of a better word 'arrested'. I was later handed over to the village magistrate who, despite my earnest plea for leniency on the grounds that starvation was my mitigation, decided that in true biblical fashion I was to suffer in an 'eye for an eye' or rather a 'hand for an apple' fashion. The very next day my sentence was passed and I lost the hand that had attempted to feed me. Justice was, in the eyes of the Crofter's and their magistrate, done and I suffered the ultimate price." explained Tobias.

"The distress you spoke of earlier Mr B'stard is a result of the disappointment I have at not coming back 'whole' and as I once was. Rather, I have come back still bearing the legacy of that fateful day" sighed Tobias. "And so Mr B'stard it was my desire and appetite for (hunger based and not sexual) a Granny Smith (the fruit and not the strangely attractive old lady of the same name who lived in the much nicer shrub next to mine) that was to be my downfall and my burden."

On hearing this B'stard's entire manner changed noticeably, as did his subsequent attitude towards Tobias.

"Then, Tobias, you will surely know that all is lost....!"

"What do you mean?" replied Tobias.

"The Journal of Albert Himmler, that's what I mean. The journal you so carefully secreted and reproduced. Surely you must know that if the prophesy is true, then he who is incomplete cannot avail themselves, nor take advantage, of the power of the sac! You are incomplete Tobias. Through an act of a seemingly innocent nature (scrumping if you will) you have denied yourself of your legacy and all that would have gone with it"

"Shit!" retorted Tobias. "Shit, Shit, Shit, Bollocks, Shit, crap and Shit!" he again retorted. This went on for a further five minutes, without pause, until Tobias had realised that B'stard spoke both truth and fact and accepted that all, indeed, was lost. That is for himself!

"What now....?" whimpered Tobias who now assumed the demeanour of a dejected and devastated man.

"What do you mean; what now?" replied B'stard. "You are lost Tobias and as such are now of no use or consequence to either myself or the Order. You cannot benefit from the scrotum, but I can." B'stard, like all B'stards that had gone before him, had seized his opportunity and usurped Tobias from his position of power at the head of the Order of the Scrotum. Or that is what B'stard would like to think. If anything Tobias had inadvertently put himself into his own predicament and as such the transfer of power was more akin to an abdication than usurping.

"I will use my innumerable wishes and stake claim to the seat of ultimate power across this land and the world beyond for I am B'stard. B'stard the Great, B'stard the Magnificent, B'stard the all Powerful, and you, my so called Lord and master, you are nothing but an unwhole and unholy aberration."

Realising that his once short-lived ally, now potential foe, had put him into a 'check-mate situation' Tobias responded

"You're B'stard-the-Thick don't you mean?"

***"What....!"*** roared B'stard. "Do you know who you are now talking to?" "Yes, yes I do. I'm talking to B'stard the Thick, B'stard the Gullible, B'stard the Complete and Utter Tit." replied Tobias in a smug and condescending way (Tobias could even be a match for David Snaith when it came to being condescending).

"You will pay for your insolence Tobias." snapped B'stard.

"Why, what you gonna do about it?" replied Tobias in a school-boy fashion as if he knew something that B'stard did not; which was true, Tobias did know something that B'stard did not and immediately went on to tell him.

"The Scrotum can only give, and has only ever been able to give, three wishes. These wishes are granted only to the holder of the scrotum. He alone can make these wishes unless his scrotum is seized (that's the monkey's and not the holders) by another before he has made his three wishes. For you see Mr B'stard, or shall I call you 'Thickie'? I deceived you and all of the Order into using your first wish to resurrect me on the promise that in return you thought you would be rewarded with an innumerable number of wishes thereafter. After you had brought me back I then intended to kill you and seize your scrotum, and that of the monkeys, and to have the two remaining wishes to myself. I would then have gone onto fulfilling my destiny and take over the world."

"What a complete and utter bastard" replied B'stard.

"I know you are, you said you are, but what am I?" Tobias childishly replied.

"You will now pay the ultimate price for your treachery Tobias Wat." said B'stard in a threatening manner. B'stard then proceeded to draw out his weapon. Holding it tight in both hands he brandished it in front of Tobias's face. Tobias stood firm as did the weapon that B'stard brandished. B'stard then slapped his weapon against Tobias's face and menacingly said

"You're gonna get it, it's what you deserve and you know it don't you? Go on say you deserve it and that you want it, bitch?"

# A Crofter's Tale (The REAL Story of The Hartlepool Monkey)

Tobias said nothing and in an act of total defiance and bravado instead simply opened his mouth to the weapon that dangled before him. This was too good an invitation to the seething B'stard and with a deep breath and an equally deep penetrative thrust he stabbed his weapon into the open mouth of Tobias Wat, bringing forth an instant gush of warm liquid. The liquid trickled from the sides of Tobias's mouth and he fell to the floor, seemingly done for. B'stard stood over the body of Tobias, clutching his still dripping weapon in both hands, vigilant of the potential for his enemy to rise up once more, seize his sword and thrust it into him.

"Now you are spent. You have lost Tobias, and you have paid with your life. You are no more." B'stard wiped clean his weapon on some Kleenex he fortuitously had secreted about his person, put it back into its sheath and turned away from Tobias as if to leave the scene and make haste his departure.

B'stard had scarcely made but two or three steps in his intended departure when all at once he heard a familiar voice. The voice was that of Tobias Wat.

"Going somewhere B'stard?" gurgled Tobias (whose mouth was still full of his own bodily fluid as he preferred to spit rather than swallow). "Don't you remember? Then you really are a thick B'stard, aren't you? You brought me back 'for now and all eternity'!"

B'stard, realising the consequences of his earlier incantation made haste once more, this time in a more hasty fashion, and left Tobias, hastily, to his own devices. Tobias chose not to pursue, knowing that sometime in the near future their paths would once again cross.

B'stard was no more, and Tobias found himself, once again, alone; he sat down to ponder his situation. He wiped the blood from his mouth which by now had stopped bleeding and, to his astonishment, had completely healed. He had at least attained one thing from the scrotum and that was his desire and wish for eternal life. This fact cheered Tobias up somewhat and he attempted to applaud himself for this achievement. However, he found it difficult to do so as he was one hand short of the clap (that's applause related and not STD related). Realising the folly of his attempted self applause he started to chuckle, it was the first time he had laughed for two hundred years.

"What's so funny?" came a voice from above him. An alert Tobias looked around. His gaze befell a familiar face.

"Gerard O'nad, is that you?" he said.

## Chapter 9
### *"Friends Reunited"*

"Indeed it is, Toby." replied O'nad. "So, you came back then?" he half asked, half stated, for it was obvious that he had.

"Yes." replied Tobias, shifting uncomfortably.

O'nad stared for a moment in disbelief at the presence which now stood before him. He could feel the mixture of opposing emotions building within him; he thought about slapping Tobias across the face, and at the same time he wanted to fling his arms, and possibly even his legs, around him to welcome him home. He did neither, but holding his emotions in check for the time being, he simply said

"Then I welcome you as a brother welcomes his kin after such a long time parted." and put out his right hand to greet his old friend, one time lover and latterly enemy. Tobias was not surprised by O'nad's terse greeting, but he did feel a pang of guilt and regret alongside his barely concealed disappointment, and so he reciprocated by offering his right hand in order to take up his old friends' greeting. He immediately withdrew the arm when he remembered that it was missing a component part.

"What in the name of....oh, Toby, my Toby what have they done to you?" cried O'nad, but he knew exactly what had happened and so immediately rushed over to his Toby and thrust his arms, and legs, around him. Tobias recoiled slightly, embarrassed at his own shortcomings, but then returned O'nad's embrace. The two stood entwined for a moment, the past forgotten briefly, as O'nad displayed his pity for what had happened to his old chum. Tobias sighed loudly and, letting out two hundred years worth of emotion, he began to sob uncontrollably on the shoulder of Gerard O'nad.

"I'm so, so sorry Gerry." he spluttered. O'nad smiled.

"Ahem!" coughed Heinny loudly as he entered the basement, "What's going on in here then?" he asked, bemused at the sight of O'nad and this weird, filth covered stranger, embracing. The aged couple separated quickly, blushing slightly.

"Ah Heinny, I didn't see you there."

"Evidently." retorted Heinny

"Allow me to introduce Heinrich Himmler, a friend of mine, Heinny, meet Mister Tobias Wat." said O'nad proudly. Heinny gasped in astonishment,

"Tobias Wat? So the prophesy has been fulfilled?"

"Well, not exactly, no." responded O'nad just as David and Julia arrived below the shop floor.

"I assume that these good people must be the Smiths, the ones foretold of in the captains' journal?" asked Tobias of O'nad

"You mean the Snaiths Toby, your long sleep must have played havoc with your memory." O'nad replied.

"No, it was definitely Sm..oww!" his utterance was curtailed by a swift kick in the shins from his partner.

"What's going on then?" asked David, "Is this Mr Dirty B'stard, he certainly looks like he could be?"

"No!" exclaimed O'nad hurriedly, "This is Toby.. er, Tobias Wat, and he has been wronged, so very gravely wronged by that awful B'stard"

"Oh? How?" responded David. "It would appear that your friend Mister B'stard has run off with the baboons' scrotum and the captains' journal, intent on making two further wishes in order to attain world power." said Watt, "Which I admit, to my eternal shame, was my own intent had things gone completely to plan"

"He's no friend of ours, is he Heinny?" asked Julia.

"So what went wrong?"

"This!" exclaimed Tobias, thrusting the stump of his right arm in Julia's direction, Julia recoiled at the raggy-ended limb; "This is what went wrong. I am not whole, I've been sent back into this breathing world scarce half made up!"

"Oh, I see." responded Julia, "So how does that affect things then?" Tobias sighed pitifully, "Only a whole person, one who is complete in every detail, can attain the power afforded by the baboons' scrotum, B'stard now has that power and we need to stop him."

"But how?" asked David becoming agitated, "He could be anywhere by now. For all we know he could have already made his two remaining wishes! That's it, it's over, it's over and we're doomed, we're all doomed!" The assembled throng, except for Tobias, beneath the shop floor of the shiny new supermarket in Hartlepool, realising that David was having some kind of panic attack, shouted, in unison *"Calm down dear!"* and began to laugh heartily at their good humour. David couldn't see the joke.

"What's so bleeding funny!" he shouted, clearly annoyed. David certainly didn't like to be the butt of the joke. The others' guffaws were reduced to the odd chuckle, nay titter, and a smiling O'nad stepped towards David.

"David, calm down." he said "All is not lost, we have the other testicle remember, the right one, for the purpose that is, it being the left one."

"That still doesn't mean B'stard won't have made his other two wishes by now though, does it?" responded David,

"Well, no, I suppose it doesn't, but B'stard is not going to waste them, as I did, he will take his time and consider his options. The left testicle will draw us to B'stard, and remember he still thinks he has innumerable wishes so he…"

"No he doesn't!" interjected Tobias, "I told him the truth!"

A momentarily stunned silence befell the room.

"You did what, Wat?" asked O'nad barely believing what he had just heard;

"I told him the truth about the prophesy, he knows he only has two wishes remaining." replied Tobias sheepishly. O'nad stood for a moment, gathering his thoughts.

"Oh well that's just spiffing, absolutely fekking spiffing! Right, come on everybody, time to go home and wait for the BBC to announce the new world order, come on, let's be having you!" in the thinly concealed manner of a certain Torquay Hotelier.

"Wait Gerry, all is not lost!" said Tobias; sarcastically O'nad responded "No, er, hang on a minute everyone, come back in, Mr Wat has a plan to save us all from world domination. Well, come on Wat, what's what? What little gem of an idea have you got in store for us all, eh? What's going to stop B'stard making his wishes, hmm?"

"He doesn't know the correct incantation" said Tobias, quietly; "Oh brilli…." O'nad began but paused again, "Brilliant!, absolutely top-hole! Why, how doesn't he have the correct incantation?" he asked excitedly, Tobias explained.

"When I copied the book I must have inadvertently turned two pages of the original document at once at some point, and so the copying became corrupted – there are a number of different incantations for various wishes as you know Gerry, the incantations I wrote in my copy are incomplete by a whole page. That page contained the world domination and eternal wealth incantations, as well as the one about a cart you can summon at will. I'd already written the resurrection incantation and numerous lesser requested orders." he paused to collect his thoughts and then continued; "I realised my mistake some time later when I revisited the original book and found that the two pages in question had been stuck together by some means." Gerard coughed nervously; "I then copied the correct incantations onto an insert which I inserted, as that is what one does with an insert, into the copied journal. Having completed my work, and shortly before I left you Gerry, I handed my copy of the journal to the growing band of followers of the new order I had created, instructing them to bury the journal with me upon my death. They built the faith and strengthened it while I grew weak from starvation. Upon my death they buried the book with me, as per my instructions, thinking it was a true document and thus thinking that they were safeguarding the future of the order. The resurrection incantation was passed through the generations, along with the coordinates for this site. They had to find me, in order to get the journal and the other incantations."

"But B'stard now has the book; he's recited them already, I just know he has, and now we're all done for!" interrupted David.

"He does, it is true, but he doesn't have the insert, for it must have fallen out during our little quarrel and I have it here!" he reached into the remains of his burial clothes' pocket and produced a tattered, muddied scrap of paper. "Upon this paper are written the incantations required by B'stard if he is to attain his goals of fabulous wealth and world domination." Everyone breathed a sigh of relief.

### *The End*

"Whoa! Hang on a cotton-picking minute. What about the remaining two wishes?" said Heinny "I'm damn sure I'm not going to let my balls being ripped off go without some kind of recompense. So, how do we get to B'stard, get my gooly case back and get me some wishes?" he continued.

"Who said anything about giving you the wishes?" uttered O'nad, "Anyway, you're not able to benefit from the magical powers are you?" he pointed out.

"No, but I can benefit in kind" said the baboon "And I want revenge!" he added.

# Chapter 10
## *"B'stard Buggered"*

Utter Dirty Terrence B'stard slinked slowly but purposefully from the Asda Supermarket, close to the headland in Hartlepool, his black leather trench coat billowing behind him in the breeze. Concealed within one of its many pockets sat the secret of his future, Heinrich Himmlers' bloodied ball bag; under his arm he carried the Captains' Journal, his new 'book of tricks' and the key to his impending power.

B'stard was still reeling from his earlier apparent good fortune, and making his mind up what to do next, as he left by the staff entrance of the store and made for his car which was parked at the front. Should he wish to be the richest man in the world? Have eternal life, or go for the biggie – that of global and universal domination? So many options, so much choice; he'd never been blessed with much in his life, attaining leadership of the Order of the Scrotum had been his greatest achievement to date and that post was voluntary and therefore unpaid. Now anything could be his.

As he rounded the corner to approach his fourteen year old fawn Ford Fiesta freestyle, he came upon the most absurd, yet annoyingly amusing, sight he had ever been witness to, some idiot had 'parked' a horse and cart directly behind his vehicle. This was all the more infuriating as it was two thirty in the morning and there were umpteen spaces available, in fact B'stards' was the only car in that section of the parking lot.

"Stupid, inconsiderate gets!" he exclaimed. Obviously it was no trouble moving it out of the way, but none the less it was an inconvenience he could do without. Once inside his vehicle he placed the journal on the passenger seat next to him, buckled up, tutted loudly at the horse and cart and fired up the engine. He breezed out of one of the disabled badge holders' spaces of the car park in no particular hurry and headed for home.

Now, what the reader needs to recall at this point is that the powers of the scrotum, in terms of the wishes it can grant, can only be realised by one who is complete. We know that Mr D B'stard to be completely complete. He is not only a complete and utter B'stard (as his nomenclature describes) but he is also complete in both body and soul. Therefore, he is part way to fulfilling his destiny and realising his wishes (whatever they may be).

We also need to recall that a wish may only be granted if the correct incantation is recited by the holder of the sac, verbatim and as it is written within the journal; Mr D B'stard has the journal, albeit a copy, and as such has access to the aforementioned incantations. It would therefore appear that Mr D B'stard has all that is required to progress his desires and fulfil the destiny of the Order of the Scrotum. Alas, the best laid plans of mice and men, particularly B'stards, are prone to spectacular failure.

It took Mr B'stard some forty minutes to travel back to his temporary abode – The Dosser's Arms Hotel – this journey should, by all rights, have taken only a couple of minutes as the hotel in question is less than half a mile from the Supermarket. The length of Mr B'stard's journey was extended due to his lack of concentration as his mind went round and round in circles, mulling over the events of the day. The actions of his mental circumnavigational procrastination led to the physical variety as he unnecessarily circled a roundabout some dozen or more times, much to the disapproval of other users of the road, which, at 2:40am, numbered two.

Finally, and quite belatedly, he drew up just outside the premises of the aforementioned hostelry. Mr B'stard, with head full of more important things, failed to realise that he had inadvertently parked his vehicle on a set of glaringly obvious, but freshly laid, double yellow lines. Without stopping to think of his prevailing actions he took the keys from the ignition, grabbed the journal, which was still resting on the passenger seat and grabbed his sac (that is the monkey's and not his own). He hastened to lock the car door then proceeded to the entrance of the welcoming but incredibly shabby abode. Once inside he headed for the flight of stairs which would take him to the second floor, on which his room was situated. The foot of the stairs stood adjacent to the hotel's reception desk which, at this time of the night, was flamboyantly and disproportionately staffed by Maureen.

All hotels, of reputable nature, employ a professional and friendly face as a front to their services and hospitality. Invariably these receptionists are female, as the stereotype dictates, or homosexual; again, as the stereotype dictates. Maureen was female but this is where the stereotypical similarities ended. Maureen was a svelte 26 stone with oily skin, riddled with acne, and equally oily ginger hair. The ginger didn't stop there either as she also had terrible gingivitis obscured, only in part, by the copious amounts of plaque coating every nominal square millimetre of her teeth (coloured black, brown, green and grey and numbering four). Maureen, unlike many of the local Crofters, took great pride in her appearance. She prided herself on her figure and took great strides to ensure she didn't 'let herself go'. Maureen would regularly snack on tripe, pig's trotters and jars of pickled onions with a pork pie stuffed in. For you see this was the only way Maureen could maintain the image she had, for years, worked to hard to attain. She was spectacularly successful in her efforts. This was Maureen's lot in life but she was willing to put up with it for the sake of maintaining her own idea of a professional and friendly approach within the hospitality industry.

Stereotypes within the hotel business also dictate that receptionists are well spoken, polite, courteous and consummately professional. Maureen was also unique to these stereotypes!

Mr D B'stard, not wishing to draw any unnecessary attention to himself, attempted to creep by the reception desk unnoticed and curtail it, with all expedience, up the wooden hill to the relative sanctuary of his room. No such luck.

"How ya doing our Terry? Ya ignorant little shit." blurted Maureen in a less than professional or friendly manner (as stereotypes would dictate).

"Bollocks!" uttered B'stard under his breath (better for it to be under his own breath than that of Maureen's as he would probably not survive such a toxic exposure).

"Oh, hello Maureen, I didn't see you there for a minute..." replied B'stard in an apologetic tone.

"Ah hope ya not avoiding me?" belched (quite literally) Maureen as she simultaneously picked the detritus of pig's trotter from between two of her four teeth whilst picking the gusset of her knickers from her enormous, bloated and cellulite ridden arse.

"Oh, absolutely not my dear, I'm just in a bit of a hurry you see." responded B'stard humbly.

"Not too busy to complete a few details in me lovely little book are ya?" asked Maureen.

"Can it wait?" asked B'stard.

"No!" roared Maureen.

"Will it take long then?" asked B'stard earnestly.

"Bout two minutes." grunted Maureen.

*"Two minutes"* thought B'stard. If this was the case then it would take B'stard to the absolute limits of endurance. For while

# A Crofter's Tale (The REAL Story of The Hartlepool Monkey)

B'stard had been staying at the hotel for some 2-3 weeks and had regular day-to-day contact with Maureen he had never been able to stomach more than, say, 15 second bursts of her terrible halitosis. Maureen was asking for 2 minutes. *"Two minutes"* he once again thought. *"That's a full 120 seconds. More importantly it's 8 times my olfactory threshold."* B'stard also knew that resistance was futile and that no matter what excuse he was to offer Maureen he would not be allowed to defer or postpone this appointment with "The devil's own satanic herd."

"Ok, Maureen." he muttered and with a deep, almost Herculean, intake of breath proceeded in the direction of Maureen and her awaiting 'form'.

"Just fill this box 'ere, then this un, followed by this, sign 'ere and then 'ere." proceeded Maureen as the seconds passed, like years, and B'stard became all the more nauseated by the arduous nature of the task. B'stard had never filled out a form of such little importance as quickly as he did for Maureen. He was amazed when he checked his timepiece to see that he had managed to do it is less than 100 seconds. This miraculous feat had, none-the-less taken its toll, for B'stard was unable to hold his breath any longer and blurted out -

"Ah, yes (puff, pant), there, it's done."

"Oh, you sound all excited there our Terry!" exclaimed Maureen.

"Just glad to be of assistance Maureen." responded B'stard backing away, and whilst maintaining his courteous approach added "And if there's anything else you'd like me to fill in Maureen...." He instantly wished he hadn't said those words, especially in that order whilst simultaneously attempting to catch his breath, for Maureen's response was predictable.

"Well, Terry, if ya offering I wouldn't mind a bit of pork sword in my sweating mound of Venus." B'stard's response to this was also predictable as he proceeded to empty the contents of his stomach in a gastric avalanche of disgust sending huge volumes of projectile vomit in the direction of Maureen. The emetic nature of her explicit request was now evident as globules of B'stards' semi-digested food cascaded down her face, hair and uniform.

"Must 'ave been summat you ate Terry!" pronounced Maureen as she nonchalantly wiped the debris from her person. B'stard wiped his face, made his apologies and bade Maureen a good night.

B'stard, safe in the relative comfort of his hotel room yet still reeling from the horrific encounter with Maureen, sat down at his bedside table and tried to compose himself. This wasn't easy as he still had the 'smell of Maureen' hounding his senses. It was as if Maureen was in the room with him; a thought that only served to make him feel even queasier. Thankfully, this wasn't the case. B'stard paused for a second, strained his rectum and let forth a potent flatus which he cupped with his left hand and drew to his nasal passageway. He then proceeded to greedily sniff at the captured flatulation. Abhorrent as this may appear it was the only way to 'tone down' the residual aromas left over from the 'Maureen experience'. *"That's better!"* sighed B'stard. *"That's much better"* and after a moment or two B'stard was feeling himself again (at this point it is fair to say that he was also feeling much better). Quietly he began to recount the day's events, not realising he was talking aloud;

"Now for some serious business. What a day. What a bloody strange day. That twat Tobias thinks he has well and truly turned me over, or so he thinks. He who laughs last. Yeah, that's how the saying goes. He who laughs last laughs longest (either that or 'he' didn't get the joke in the first place). But I didn't see Tobias laughing when I saw him last. No, I'm the one with the monkey's scrotum and I'm the one with the two remaining wishes. Tobias Wat will be sorry when I've made my two wishes. He'll wish he'd never been born. But wait, he can't wish that as I've got all the wishes and he's got none."

By now B'stards personal utterance grew more into a tirade of imbecilic rantings. He grew more and more frustrated and furious over how Tobias had tried to 'stitch him up'. "Right, there's not a moment to lose. My fate and destiny are now at hand and I'll get my just desserts."

What happened next will, in the eyes of the reader, appear somewhat impetuous but you must appreciate that B'stard's emotions were at their height at this point and as such common sense and considered forethought has escaped him.

"I'll make my wishes now and I'll set myself upon the road to world domination." Clutching the monkey's scrotum in one hand he closed his eyes and uttered "Make me rich, rich beyond my wildest dreams and make my life everlasting so that I know not what it is to ever be poor again. These are my wishes and this is my desire."

B'stard remained still, with eyes closed. He dared not open his eyes just yet and instead took time to reflect on the wishes he'd just made. He figured that someone who was immortal and had unending riches would surely find his place as world leader, nay, total universal ruler. The logic appeared to be water-tight. He could no longer bear the excitement which was welling up inside him. He tentatively opened one eye and gazed around the room. He then opened his other (second and last) eye so as to see if there was anything different. There was not. He thought nothing of what he observed around the room thinking instead that immortality and unending riches were something that could not obviously be seen. His excitement failed to dissipate and he was therefore convinced he had been granted that which he had wished for. But how now do I test? That was the question now within B'stard's thoughts.

It then came to him in a flash of inspiration (albeit not altogether original). "I'll go to the cash point and check the balance of my current account. The ATM machine will surely go into overload when it's forced to calculate the balance of my current,

# A Crofter's Tale (The REAL Story of The Hartlepool Monkey)

cleared funds." he laughed to himself. B'stard's laugh was reminiscent of that of an old Hollywood B movie baddie, say, Ming the Merciless from the Adventures of Flash Gordon. He was now truly entering into the spirit of taking on the guise of merciless despot. This further excited B'stard until he could hold his excitement no longer. He retired to the lavatory at this point to 'relax in a gentleman's way'.

After his act of onenism he pulled himself together (which involved pulling his pants back up from his ankles and onto his waist) and grabbed his key to make haste to his vehicle, parked just outside the hotel.

He closed the door of his room behind him and skipped along the corridor and down the flight of stairs which would bring him to the reception area.

"Maureen!!!!" he uttered to himself. "She'll be there, the fat old trout". (It was quite unfair of B'stard to make this remark as Maureen is actually only nineteen) Maureen was indeed at reception but B'stard's luck was in as it was one of her many 'breaks'. B'stard observed her devouring a 'Cornish Pasty' (well, several actually) still covered with his by now crusting stomach contents. It was safe to proceed. B'stard had, over the weeks he'd stayed at the Dosser's Arms Hotel, noticed that Maureen never lifted her head from the 'troughing' position whilst on a 'break' no matter how fervently one might attempt to attract her attention.

B'stard walked past Maureen. Maureen was totally oblivious to his presence.

Once outside, B'stard made for his vehicle which was parked just around the corner. As he approached his car he espied a figure which seemed to be looming over the bonnet. B'stard thought this to be rather curious and his suspicions lead him to believe that someone was in the process of "Touching A Dog's Arse" (this being an anarchic euphemism for the legal term of car-theft – Taking and Driving Away or TADA. This euphemism has since been modified and replaced with Taking Without Owners Consent or TWOCing). B'stard yelled out at the ominous character

"Oi, what do you think you're doing?"

The shadowy character moved position and now stood perfectly upright besides the vehicle. The image of the person, who stood before B'stard, now became all the more clear. B'stard's first observations were that the mysterious character was wearing some type of uniform. He also observed that he was brandishing a notebook of some sort and that hovering above the note book was a writing implement held in the person's leather clad hand. It then came to B'stard in a dawn of realisation, albeit a slightly delayed one. It was a Traffic Warden.

"Is thith your vehicle thir?" lisped the Traffic Warden.

"Yeth, er, I mean yes it is." responded B'stard.

"Then you will no doubt be aware that you are illegally parked?" said the Traffic Warden as he pointed to the double yellow lines on which B'stard's car was sited. B'stard, still brimming with confidence at his new found fortune and immortal state, proceeded to lambaste the Warden.

"So, what the hell are you going to do about it then you gormless looking freak?"

"I'll tell you what I'm going to do thir, I'm going to give you a fixthed penalty ticket, that'th what." replied the equally confident Warden. B'stard was furious at the suggestion offered by the Warden. How dare he talk to me this way he thought? B'stard then lunged at the Warden and grabbed the notebook from his hands.

"Thir, you cannot obthruct a Warden in hith dutieth" reacted the Warden as he attempted to retrieve his notebook from B'stard. B'stard, not willing to yield possession of the aforementioned article pushed the Warden with all his might. This sent the Warden crashing to the ground. B'stard stood over the Warden and roared

"Now sod off before I do you some real damage!"

"Thyit, you've really done it now thir, I'm calling the poleeth!" threatened the Warden.

"Do it then you little shit!" The Traffic Warden did as he'd threatened and called for immediate assistance via his two-way radio device. Unfortunately, the assistance was not immediately forthcoming and, in fact, it took some 30 minutes before any signs of the local constabulary were to be seen. During this half-hour period B'stard proceeded to pummel the poor defenceless Warden with his trusty blunt weapon.

Finally, the sirens of the police car could be heard and B'stard ceased the relentless beating of the Warden. He looked up and saw the police car come to a screeching halt, after which two rather burly looking officers emerged and approached B'stard.

"Evenin' all, what's all this then, let's be 'aving you!" asserted one of the officers in a typically stereotypical way. B'stard, still high on bravado raged

"You'll never take me alive copper, do you hear. I'm on top of the world, top of the world." Now, in order for the police to 'never take him alive' this would imply that they would have to take him 'dead' yet B'stard thought he was immortal and so he was surely embarrassing himself by making such a contradictory statement. Also, it didn't help the fact that his threat was uttered in a James Cagney (White Heat) style accent. You would be right in thinking that B'stard had, in some way, gone slightly over the top in his act of 'Hollywood' bravado. Thankfully, the police failed to make the connection due, in the main, to the fact that B'stard had stopped short of carrying out a song and dance routine to go with his Cagney-esque persona.

"Do you know who you are talking to?" snarled B'stard.

"Yes, yes we do. It would appear we are talking to a rather nasty little bastard." replied one of the officers.

"Ah, so you've heard of me have you?" retorted B'stard. The officers, on hearing this, turned to one another and stared in a curiously bemused fashion (for reasons that should, by now, be obvious to the reader).

"Calm down sir." said one of the officers as he approached B'stard. The tones of the officer's voice suggesting empathy and a willingness to help in this unfortunate set of circumstances. B'stard remained resolute as he stood in close proximity to the two officers. One of them began to talk to B'stard and as such distracted him from the other. This was to prove a decisive move for the Boys in Blue. ***Thud!**,* went a truncheon right across B'stard's knapper. *"Ouch!"* reacted B'stard as he was sent crashing to the floor in an unconscious state. Strangely, at this point the skies darkened, clouds dissipated and the heavens were filled with a myriad stars and simultaneously a flock of canaries came swooping in and began circling the head of the unconscious B'stard. The police officers knelt at B'stard's side to make sure that the 'reasonable force' they'd employed had not served to unreasonably kill him. All appeared fine as the two inspected B'stard for vital signs. The only thing of note, which was observed by the officers, was that a large swelling had appeared where the truncheon had come crashing down. The swelling was approximately 4 inches high and bright red. It also began pulsating and throbbing, curious!

# Chapter 11
## *"From Immortality to Incarceration"*

Justice was served upon B'stard at the Magistrate's court as quickly as the policeman's truncheon had come crashing down on his cranium only the day before. The Magistrates had taken all of the associated evidence and the mitigating factors behind B'stard's involvement in the illicit misdemeanours and had served up his sentence.

Strangely, despite the Traffic Warden being in a coma which, according to the medical experts, he would not be likely to recover from (and if he did he would live the remainder of his life a tetraplegic) the sentence passed upon B'stard was quite lenient. Expecting the sentence to be passed in 'years' B'stard was shocked to hear that he was to be given a custodial sentence of just 7 days, with costs amounting to £20:49 for damage to police property – i.e the truncheon (which had somehow been snapped in two and was found to be contaminated by human blood and fragments of cranial matter). Coincidentally, the Magistrate who passed this sentence was in fact a stand-in for the usual Magistrate who was away on annual leave. The Magistrate who had passed this 'merciful' sentence needed to do the overtime as he needed to find funds to pay off a parking ticket he picked up from a short-tongued, short arsed Warden only the week before.

B'stard's head was throbbing from the effects of the coshing he'd received the day before and he could scarcely believe his luck on hearing the sentence; and so it was, the sentence was passed, B'stard passed out, a member of the jury passed wind and Mr Goldstein (the Court Clerk) left the courtroom to visit his synagogue to celebrate Passover.

B'stard, once again, stirred from an unconscious state to find himself laid prostrate on a crude bed within the confines of his new 'temporary abode' – his prison cell. He dared not open his eyes at this point as his head was still throbbing. Instead, B'stard listened intently to the sounds around him. Firstly, he perceived the sound of a key in its lock. He recognised this as the sound of the 'Screw' securing the door of his cell. He was locked in, his sentence had begun! B'stard lay quiet for a few seconds more as he started to think about his predicament. His thoughts were then quickly and abruptly interrupted by a gravelly voice that boomed the words;

# A Crofter's Tale (The REAL Story of The Hartlepool Monkey)

*"Who's a pretty boy then?"*

B'stard released a sigh of impending doom. *"That's it he thought, I'm in prison, in a cell with a raving homosexual and I'm about to get buggered, typical."* Again the voice boomed the words;

*"Who's a pretty boy then? Come to Daddy."*

*"Shit"* thought B'stard *"I'm going to get rimmed by the Daddy, the main man, the head honcho. This is absolutely sodding typical."* Then, incongruously, the next sound that B'stard heard was the sweetest tweeting and chirruping of a small bird. B'stard slowly opened his eyes and set his gaze upon his 'cell buddy'. His buddy sat in a chair next to a bird cage which contained a delightful and chirpy looking budgerigar. *'Thank Christ for that!'* thought B'stard. *'He was talking to the bird.'* B'stard breathed a sigh of relief and raised himself from his bed to face his cell mate.

*"Hi"* said B'stard groggily.

*"Oh, you're awake then I see."* responded his mate. B'stard looked his partner up and down. He was a well-made man probably about 14 stones and 6 foot tall. His most noticeable feature was that of a turban which he was wearing on his head (as is the tradition with turban wearers).

"Ah, you must be a Sikh?" asked B'stard.

"How did you know that? Who's been talking? How do you know so much about me?" the man replied.

"Oh, it's just a little hunch." replied B'stard. With that the man got to his feet. B'stard's initial estimations about his cell-mates height were confirmed to be quite wrong. He was more like 5 foot 2 inches and almost bent double.

"A little hunch you say. I'd like to see you carry this monstrous carbuncle around with you!" and as he said this he turned to show B'stard his hunchback.

"Ah, sorry there, I didn't mean any offence. What I had meant to say was that it was your turban which led me to the conclusion of your faith or religion."

"Oh, I see. Then I suppose you're forgiven then." replied the Sikh (He was a Sikh. Why?; because he wore a turban).

"Let me introduce myself, I'm Anul, Anul Abu-Sar."

"Anul who?" replied B'stard.

"Abu-Sar, spelt A-B-U-hyphen-S-A-R." responded Anul. B'stard thought to himself that no matter how his new found friend's name was pronounced there was no getting away from the fact that he was sat in the presence of a Sikh called Anal Abuser! This worried B'stard immensely and he immediately wondered if the earlier reference as to "who was a pretty boy" was indeed aimed at B'stard or the Budgie. B'stard hoped and prayed that it was the latter.

"Ah, my name's Bast…. er, Terry, nice to meet you." Quite why B'stard chose to offer up his middle name is a mystery. Perhaps it was offered up so as not to cause any offence or indeed give Anul any reason to think he was being funny or facetious.

"What you in for then Anul?" asked B'stard.

"Grande Necromancy and Grievous Buggery." responded Anul.

*'Oh, fuck!'* thought B'stard, as his worst nightmares started to unfold. "Oh, I see. What did you get for that then?" asked B'stard earnestly.

"A shitty dick and 10 years." said Anul.

"Oh, is that the time?" said B'stard as he looked at his watch, which was showing 4:30pm. "It's nearly my bedtime. I think I'll get off to bed if that's Ok with you?"

"Whatever." replied Anul.

B'stard, fully clothed, entombed himself in his blanket, encasing every inch of his body with the rough Hessian cover. The only part of B'stard that was visible were his eyes, which he fixed upon Anul until such time as he observed him fall asleep. This was some seven hours later. Anul could be heard snoring loudly as the hands on B'stards' watch approached midnight and the end of day

# A Crofter's Tale (The REAL Story of The Hartlepool Monkey)

one in his prison cell. B'stard dared not fall asleep for fear of what might become of him at the hands of Abu-Sar.

When B'stard was absolutely sure that Anul was in a deep sleep he released himself from his cocoon slipped his hands into his trouser pocket and grabbed his ball bag (the monkey's) and the journal. Quite why the prison authorities had allowed B'stard to keep his sac and little book were unknown. Perhaps they thought them to be of little threat to his welfare or life as they had never come across anyone hanging themselves by their scrotum. Though, if you were to look at some web-sites on the internet I'm sure there's one out there which would prove this event to be common place in some circles. Also, they (the prison authorities) may have mistaken B'stard's little journal as some form of religious book and as such allowed him to retain it on the grounds of them being a diverse and inclusive and politically correct organisation. Anyway, B'stard had his sac and his journal and there was just about enough ambient light in the cell to allow him to peruse the pages.

B'stard read the introduction. The same old stuff; it was the doctrine of the Order of the Scrotum, which told of how the prophecy would one day allow the Order to take control of the world.

"Yeah, Tobias Wats' words; the words of a liar. He well and truly buggered me on this one, but I guess he got his comeuppance, as I now hold the sac and I've gotten the wishes he'd hoped he'd have." B'stard skipped much of this section as he knew it all already and anyway no-one ever reads the introduction of a book with the possible exception of this one.

He then moved onto the section which, in descriptive detail, described how best to use the sac for the purpose of making the wishes. B'stard had never really read this section in any great depth as, by his own admission, he was never a strong reader, preferring instead to look at the 'pretty pictures' (of which the journal had very few, in fact none). Given that B'stard had an abundance of time on his hands, what with being imprisoned and all, he decided to give this section his full attention. After all he had made his wishes already but was curious as to why they appeared not to be taking effect yet, and he felt the urge to know how they might eventually manifest themselves. What B'stard read shocked him to the core. He'd dropped an enormous bollock (sorry for the pun there). The journal talked of wishes only coming true for the holder of the sacred scrotum if the incantations, held within the journal, were recited correctly. No other way would be an acceptable way to make these wishes come true however hard the holder of the sac tries. This is why the sac and the journal are symbiotically matched. B'stard immediately realised his error. He had made his wishes simply by asking for them. He had asked for them in a way which was removed from the critical use of the appropriate incantation. He read on.

He read the lines "For a list of incantations please turn to pages 879-904". You will now possibly appreciate why B'stard had failed to read the journal in its entirety as the tome was 'mammoth' in its gargantuosity, and page 879 was, in fact, only part way through chapter 6 of a 24 chapter journal. You may also find it strange that such a large volume of text could be printed in such a 'pocket-sized' way (though B'stard does wear combat trousers which account, in part, for the portable nature of the book).

"Bugger!" whispered B'stard to himself. "I'm neither wealthy nor immortal. Let's hope that the appropriate incantation can be found in this journal of mine." B'stard quickly flicked the pages to the relevant sections and hurriedly scanned the pages within to find the incantations for wealth and immortality. He could not find them. He quickly realised that there appeared to be some pages missing, though the copied script was numbered correctly. He surmised that these pages were the ones that held the incants he so longed to read. Seemingly, with all hopes and wishes dashed B'stard began to feel deflated. He wouldn't now get what he desired most.

"But wait!" he said to himself. "There are 'other' incantations. Perhaps there're some equally useful ones I can exploit!" B'stard read on. He perused each incantation one by one in an attempt to find one to his liking. "Now, let's see."

The first incantation B'stard came upon was one for *"The ability to grow the finest root crop vegetables the world has ever seen"*. This one came with a guarantee that would ensure that the holder of the wish would be all conquering in the field of market gardening. B'stard immediately dismissed this option as he was a 'chips' man and despised anything that was green and meant for human consumption.

The second incantation was equally dismissed by B'stard as he thought it to be completely useless, especially given his desires were that of world domination. The second incantation was *"The ability to become a master of illusion and deceiver of the eye"*, potentially this incantation could have benefits, specifically in attracting the eyes and ears of the political 'movers and shakers' though B'stard concluded that there were always going to be people able to 'see through' any illusion or deception, and those who possessed such insight usually already had the eyes and ears of the power brokers, so he decided not to avail himself of this option.

The third incantation was even less promising thought B'stard. *"The ability to use a cork screw in strange and mysterious ways"* B'stard instantly rebuffed this option also as he thought his street credibility would be seriously compromised if all he could do was to be mysterious with such a utensil.

By this stage B'stard was losing all faith in the journal and the inane incantations it held within. For a brief moment he seriously considered tossing the book into the garbage. However, he read on and eventually became pleased that he had done so for the two remaining incantations were "right up his alley".

The fourth incantation read: *"The ability to use a cloak of invisibility at will, especially for deeds of a devious and heinous nature."* "Brilliant, I'm definitely having that one!" he chirped to himself.

Now, if the reader thinks that this incantation was good then you ain't seen nothing yet. For the fifth and final incantation was the best of the lot (granted the last two were the best of a seriously, poor bunch, but you can only have what the journal offers). The fifth incantation offered *"The ability to summon an Army of the Dead and have supreme control over them, again for deeds relating to a devious a heinous nature."* "Brilliant, I'll have that one as well!" said B'stard.

With ball bag in hand he tightly squeezed the Simian Scrotal Sac and recited the first (being the fourth incantation).

**"Now you see me,**
**Now you don't,**
**Cloak me from view,**
**So others won't"**

The incantation was complete and so the wish became reality. B'stard could turn himself on and turn himself off. He was very much used to turning himself on but this time it was different. All he had to do to activate the ability was to utter the words *"Just like that!"* (although a condition of the incantation, when B'stard had read the 'small print' was that the utterance was to be conducted in the style of Tommy Cooper whilst simultaneously offering out his hands, palms faced down, in a back and forth motion). B'stard tried this and followed the conditions to the letter of the incantations instructions. *"Just like that!"* said B'stard and immediately he became invisible. *"Cool"* thought B'stard. He repeated the instruction to find that he was visible once more. Time and time again he went over the phrase switching from visible to

# A Crofter's Tale (The REAL Story of The Hartlepool Monkey)

invisible each time. If a 'Screw' happened upon his cell during their nightly rounds and over-heard these whispering from within they might mistake the occupant for some form of wannabe variety artiste. Either way it was unlikely to rouse any suspicion.

Happy with his first wish and confident that his new found ability would be of use to him; soon B'stard progressed to his second (that is to say fifth) and final incantation.

B'stard read the following incantation:

> *"Army of the Dead,*
> *Get out of your bed,*
> *Do as I say,*
> *And follow what is said"*

Now, just as with B'stard's first (fourth) incantation so this one had its conditions. B'stard was also required to read the words "Byddin am y marw". Which B'stard would later discover is the Welsh for "Army of the Dead". He was also advised not to ever summon the 'Army' in an enclosed space (e.g. a prison cell) for fear of catastrophic, if not fatally claustrophobic, events. All B'stard needed to do to summon his Army, in more appropriate surroundings, was to say "Isn't it not look you, there's lovely" Which B'stard thought to be a little peculiar, but none the less assigned these words to his memory.

"That's it. Victory is mine. I will have my destiny!" uttered B'stard. "Tobias Wat thought he had shafted me when I resurrected him, only to discover his treacherous plans. I, myself, thought I was shafted having found myself incarcerated in these prison walls but it is I who will have the last laugh, and I who will laugh longest."

B'stard grew more and more excited at his latest fortunes and he jumped out of bed with an impulse of nervous energy shouting "Who's buggered now?" This was to prove fateful as

B'stard disturbed the Budgies cage and it came crashing down on the hard floor of the cell with an enormous clatter. This woke Anul, who was not best pleased.

"I'll tell you who's buggered!" raged the Sikh as he grabbed B'stard by the love handles and proceeded to mount him. Despite B'stard's every efforts he could not, under the circumstances, bring himself to utter the words "Just like that!"

# Chapter 12

## *"The Enrolment of Anul"*

Following his severe rogering of B'stard, Anul finally released his vice-like grip on his victim and B'stard, angered by the violation of his person, began hitting out at Anul, raining down blows upon the Sikh sodomite with a fury he never knew he had within him. His rage seemed endless and the power of his blows became stronger as he realised that Anul was not fighting back, nor was he defending himself, save for holding onto his now flaccid member and its accompanying appendages.

"What's the matter with you, you fucking pervert?" B'stard screamed at him. Hunched over the edge of the metal framed bottom bunk bed, not because he was cowering but because it was his natural position, Anul quietly and slowly said

"I'm sorry my friend, I don't know what happened to me!" B'stard screamed back;

"You're sorry, are ya? I'll make you fucking sorry mate, you don't know who you're messing with here!" Anul responded by uttering what B'stard thought were the most pathetic words he had ever heard;

"You hurt my Bobby!"

"Hurt your bobby? Hurt your bobby?" he could barely contain a giggle at the thought that this turban wearing hunchback called his knob 'Bobby',

"I should hope I did hurt it, you shouldn't go sticking it up strangers' arses then, should you? You almost ripped my arse open, you filthy get!"

Anul looked at B'stard perplexed.

"You don't understand." he muttered, a tear sliding down his cheek; and with that he crouched on the floor of the cell and picked up the lifeless body of his pet budgie,

"You hurt my Bobby!" he repeated offering up the body of his bird to B'stards' face. B'stard nonchalantly brushed his hand away and the yellow bird fell from Anuls' gentle grip and slumped to the floor.

"So fucking what?" said B'stard heartlessly.

"Why, you evil basta.." began Anul as he made a lunge at B'stard. B'stard almost instinctively thrust his forearms in front of him and uttered the magic words

*"Just like that!"* He was instantly invisible and able to sidestep the oncoming Anul who crashed unceremoniously, hump first, into the cell wall.

"What the fuc...?" he began to say, but found his words cut off by the hand which now gripped his cheeks together (those on his face). Trouble was the 'hand' was not visible, he just felt it. Felt the pain of the fingernails digging into his bearded flesh.

"Not so big now, eh, Mister Abu-Sar?" It was B'stards' voice, but he could not see him, he could, however, feel the blood trickling down his ravaged cheeks. B'stard let go, wiping his bloodied hand on Anuls' prison issue shirt.

"What are you?" asked Anul, terrified. B'stard simply said

"I am your worst nightmare!" and with that he punched his humped cell mate so hard he almost broke his own knuckles. Anul had no defence mechanism with which to avoid the unseen hand and took the fisting full in the face. He screamed as his already bloodied cheek cracked and a fresh gush of blood burst forth from the resulting broken nose. B'stard followed this up with an upper cut and Anul bit right through his own tongue, the bottom teeth connecting with his upper set so powerfully that several of them re-embedded themselves into their opposing gum. The resulting hideous bloodied grin made him look as though he had the fangs of a cat.

"Thop, thop, pleathe." he gurgled through the bloody mess of his face. B'stard thopped, I mean stopped. He took a step back from his, now cowering, victim intending to relaunch his violent onslaught from a different angle, but for some reason he found that he no longer wished to hurt him. The pitiful sight of the hump-backed short arsed homosexual rapist scrabbling on the cell floor looking for his dead pet budgie was enough for tonight it seemed, either that or the thought of extending his seven day sentence into life imprisonment for murder, brought him to his senses and he uttered the words *"Just like that!"* whilst simultaneously moving his down-turned palms back and forth; he was instantly visible again and saw the fear in his cell mates face. Anul began to sob uncontrollably, in grief for his dead bird, and pain from the beating he had just taken.

"Let that be a lesson to you, you dirty rotten get!" said B'stard. "No one bums me and gets away with it, you will see how powerful I can get in due course mister Abu-Sar!" he continued. Through blood, tooth and fragments of cheek bone Anul weakly asked again "What are you?" B'stard thought for a moment, relishing the grip of fear he now held over the beaten fellow before him, realising the immense power of his cloak of invisibility for the first time, he smiled a sinister smile and responded "My name is B'stard, Mister Dirty B'stard and I am all powerful, you may call me sir, though I suppose you'll have to call me 'thir' or thomething thimilar!" he chuckled to himself. "Bow to me now you perverse creep, kiss the feet of your new master, B'stard the invincible, and invisible; B'stard the master of deception, soon to be leader of the world, if not the universe!" and he proceeded to relate to his beaten cell mate the entire story of how he came by his powers and how he would one day soon make his powers known to the world in order to create a power struggle which would lead, ultimately, to his enthronement at the helm of the world stage. He relayed all there was to know about the Order of the Scrotum, Tobias Wats' resurrection, and how he had usurped power from him; and the baboon's scrotum which afforded him his powers.

Once he had finished this epic tale he noticed a shift in bravado of his new servile Sikh cell mate. Imperceptible at first, but gradually Anul began to talk to B'stard as though it was he who had the upper hand. Confused by this shift B'stard sought to regain control and commanded Anul to bow before him once more.

"You can go and fuck yourthelf Mithter Bathtard, I will not bow to one who murderth my Bobby."

**"What?"** roared B'stard "How dare you, you cre...." he began, but found his sentence severed by Anul who bellowed back at B'stard

"How'th it going to look Mithter Bathtard, when you atthain world dominathion, and I pop up to announth to the worldth preth that we enjoyed an anal liaithon whiltht tharing a thell in prithon?"

"What?" said B'stard unable to decipher the newly short tongued humpty dumpty before him, Anul sighed.

"I thaid, what are you going to look like when I thteal your victory parade by announthing to the world that you're a bummer and that we thared a clothe relathionthip here in our thell?"

B'stard pondered this thought for a moment before responding.

"I could always kill you right now."

"You could." replied Anul, "but then you'd be in here for life, and you'd mith your opportunity to gain world dominathion, at leatht whilsth you're thtill young enough to enjoy it " he paused to wipe away more blood from his mouth and then said "Tho you thee, not only am I a pain in your arthe in prithon, I'll be one on the outthide too! I think I have the upper hand here!"

B'stard became concerned by the Sikh's threat. He didn't want to ruin his chances of using his wishes to their fullest effect – in order to reach, and take control of the world stage – but he also didn't want to concede anything to this cowardly, bloodied, hunch backed gay rapist either. Anul broke his thoughts;

"I could help you with your quetht for world domination"

"How?" responded B'stard "You're in here, and anyway I have an army of my own to help me with my quest, I don't need a hunchback slowing me down."

Anul replied "Why do you think I'm in a holding cell on the remand wing? Me, Anul Abu-Sar, the great buggerer and shagger of dead people, think about it?"

B'stard had to admit he had thought it strange that such a violent criminal, convicted of Grande Necromancy and Grievous Buggery, should be in such a low security part of the prison, Anul continued to enlighten him;

"I'm due for a parole board hearing tomorrow. I've been in here for five yearth and my brief reckonth that, with good behaviour, I'll be releathed on lithence. Onthe out, I could be a friend, ath oppothed to a conthtant threat. I could help you."

B'stard had his doubts, but given the circumstances, and the potential threat posed by Anul's knowledge he was forced to capitulate and so he offered the Sikh the chance to help him command his army.

"Oh I don't know about leading an army, I've never had command like that before." responded Anul;

"Oh, it'll be easy." retorted B'stard "I have complete control over them. I will simply order my Army of the Dead to follow you, it'll be ea...."

"Army of the Dead, you say?" interrupted Anul questioningly.

"Er, yes. I have the power to summon an army of the dead at will, and they will hel..." his words were cut off once more by an over enthusiastic response from his cell mate;

"I'll do it!" squealed Anul. B'stard didn't notice the immense glee, and obvious excited delight, in Anuls' acceptance.

# Chapter 13
## *"Lucky for some"*

Sadly, not for this book.

# Chapter 14
## *"The Summoning of McNad"*

As B'stard was leaving the supermarket car park, David and Julia Snaith, O'nad and Tobias were emerging from the basement. Heinny was already at the doorway watching out for potential threats. Had he used the rear exit of the store, he would have seen B'stard and could have, quite easily, confronted him, thus ending our epic tale. Unfortunately (for him) he did not and so fortunately (for us) the race began to capture B'stard and stop him making whatever wishes he could find that might prove worthy replacements for the missing ones.

As the strange charabanc pulled out of the car park they passed a shining new Ford Focus, the two occupants of which stared, open mouthed, at the horse and cart carrying the odd collection of muddied folk. The beautiful model-like, female occupant, in the driving seat, turned to her Adonis-like, muscle-bound ex marine husband in the passenger seat.

"David, did you see that?" she asked.

"I did Julia, I did. Looks like the gypsies are back in town, and now they've got a pet monkey." David had a strange aversion to anything equine and shuddered at the sight of the horse and cart. Julia laughed, tossing back her golden locks and heaving her ample bosoms forward, proceeding into the car park to get on with answering the police call about a break in at the supermarket they jointly managed. An officer greeted them; "Hello Mr and Mrs Smith." he said.

O'nad whipped his mare into action and soon they were heading, at no great speed, to Heinny's temporary home. No one spoke on the journey. Forty five minutes later they arrived at the prestigious Premier Night Lodge, parked up their horse and cart and alighted from it. Once everyone was safely removed O'nad clapped his hands three times in quick succession, and the vehicle disappeared into the atmosphere, as it went O'nad gently stroked the muzzle of his beloved horse.

The odd-looking crew made haste for the entrance to the hotel and, once inside were greeted heartily by the reception staff who, being professional and courteous, ignored their dishevelled appearance and booked them into individual rooms, even offering to provide a cage for their 'pet monkey.' "That's quite alright young lady. A double room will suffice for me, thank you very much." responded Heinny.

Strangely, Julia had asked for a single room stating that she had a migraine coming on and needed to rest, alone. David didn't seem at all perturbed by her actions and instead looked forward to

# A Crofter's Tale (The REAL Story of The Hartlepool Monkey)

a decent rest without his constantly snoring and fidgety wife beside him.

Heinny assisted Julia up to her room and stood with her in the doorway, he gently brushed her cheek.

"Get some rest Julia." he said.

Julia's thoughts drifted to a time when they could be together, oh how she longed to allow him access, and indeed even let him in her room. She quickly snapped back to reality when she heard the lift doors opening and her husband and the others stumbling out in search of their own rooms. Heinny winked at her, curtailing his own longing, for the time being.

In the second floor corridor O'nad arranged for everyone to meet back up in four hours, to give them time to freshen up and possibly even get some sleep.

Once inside his room O'nad contemplated the events of the last few hours since his arrival in Hartlepool; the sight which had greeted him in the basement of the supermarket; the mixed emotions of being reunited with his one time lover Tobias Wat, the one who began this whole sordid chase through his greed and jealousy of what O'nad had, and the one he felt so sorry for that forgiveness was instant after discovering he'd been thwarted, by B'stard, in his attempts to seize power from the scrotum. But what now, how could they get to B'stard in time to stop him?

O'nad knew that the journal contained corrupted versions of the world domination and wealth incantations, but he also knew that there were hundreds of other incantations which could be turned to the benefit of B'stard. They had to get to him before he made his wishes.

His thoughts were interrupted by a light tapping on the door of his room. Being a cautious person he checked through the spy-hole of the door to see who it was before unlocking it and allowing entry to his baboon friend.

"I've been thinking, O'nad." he said as he entered the room and closed the door behind him. "What if we're too late? What if

B'stard has made his wishes already and realised his mistake, he'll now be frantically searching the journal for an incantation of some use to him, and you and I both know that there are many in that journal which could be turned to his evil?"

O'nad motioned for his friend to sit whilst he tried to answer the questions and calm the baboon's fears; Heinny complied with the unspoken request.

"If B'stard has tried the incorrect incantations then he'll be finding out, some time soon, that they haven't worked, and we know that they will not work for they are corrupt, what we don't know is whether or not they work in the fashion of the corruption – so he could be halfway through the incantation for immortality, turn the page and finish off with the end of an incantation for free food for the rest of his life. Do you see?" he asked, Heinny nodded.

"If the wish has worked he will not have to pay for food for the rest of his life, but he'll think that he has immortality and so might, just might, do something to prove his new found power and end up dead, or seriously injured. We have to hope that this is the case and that, by ending the incantation with the wrong words, he cancels the use of the wish in the first place – so he doesn't get anything, no free food, no immortality, no wish."

"But will the wish still be available?" asked Heinny,

"That, my friend, is the unknown, we will just have to wait and see." replied O'nad.

After Heinny had left his room, seemingly convinced of the theory he had imparted, O'nad sat on the edge of his bed, took out of his bag a pair of shiny, diamante encrusted red shoes, of the sort worn by Dorothy on the Wizard of Oz, slipping them onto his feet he then reached for the mangled, blood soaked orb that had once been attached to Heinny, and closed his eyes. He knew what he now had to do to find the whereabouts of B'stard.

Talking aloud, but in a whispering voice so as not to be heard by the others, and whilst simultaneously clicking his heels together three times, he began to recite an incantation he had hoped he would never have to use, but one that he had trusted to memory just in case, he firmly squeezed the baboons' left testicle and said;

*"Power of the teste bring forth to me*
*the one who will find my enemy"*

Nothing happened, though this did not surprise him, as many of the incantations from the journal produced little in the way of evidence of their success. He simply placed the testicle on the bed beside him and waited. After a short while the bruised ball began to visibly vibrate, O'nad watched intently. As the vibrations grew stronger from within the mangled plum, he could see that it was slowly, almost imperceptibly, changing shape. Two tiny bumps appeared on opposite sides of the sacred orb, the remaining epidydimal tissue began to slowly curl itself around its base, or head, and as it did so it took on the form of a Mr Whippy ice cream. At the opposite end a further two bumps had appeared and O'nad now could see the emergence of actual limbs from the gooly. The first two bumps now began to take on the shape of arms and, on the lower set he could just make out tiny toes. He was not, in any way, shocked or surprised to see the unfolding metamorphosis, for he knew that he was soon to be in the presence of the orienteering capability of the left testicle, which had so far been unused.

Moments later the first signs of a face appeared on the ever growing orb, two sealed eyes and a mouth appeared to form in a split second. At the same time as the mouth opened, he could see that the arms and legs of the bollock had now fully formed; one of the eyes opened and O'nad saw the tiny pupil contract at the bright light of the room, it instantly closed again.

*"See you ya bassa, turn oot the light before ya blind me, ya Sassenach!"*

O'nad smiled and dimmed the light sufficiently to allow him to see whilst not hurting the eyes of his new companion.

"Welcome Mr McNad." he said.

*"Ah'll gee ya welcome ya freak, what d'ya thank ya doin' spoilin' ma sleep by squeezin' the fuckin' life oot a me?"* responded the angry looking McNad.

"I am in need of your magical capabilities, Mr McNad. I need you to find the one known as Mister Dirty Terrence B'stard, for he has stolen your home, and your brother." said O'nad.

*"Oh he has, has he noo? Ah'll teach that bassa a lesson he'll nivver forget, but first ah'll need a wee dram!"*

O'nad duly complied with the testicles request and took a small bottle of Scotch from the mini bar, he reached for one of the delightful plastic cups stocked in such hotel rooms.

*"Di nah bother wi a glass, bonny lad, jus gimme the bottle!"* O'nad handed the bottle to McNad who stood for the first time and, gripping it with both hands, lifted it to his tiny lips. As he lifted the bottle he unbalanced himself and fell back on to the bed still holding the bottle firmly, though spilling the contents over himself and the bedspread. Luckily for him he had landed under the neck of the bottle and proceeded to greedily gulp the spilling contents. O'nad observed the bizarre spectacle of a testicle greedily guzzling cheap scotch from a bottle bigger than itself and couldn't help the ensuing guffaw. Breaking free of the torrent of liquor momentarily McNad screamed at him

*"Don't you go laughin' at me now, or ah'll break yer legs, yer wee Irish upstart. Do yer want ma help or not?"*

"I'm sorry." uttered O'nad guiltily.

McNad returned his attention to the flow of whisky, lifting the base of the bottle with his legs to maintain the flow as the bottle emptied. Once finished he thrust aside the empty container and stood once more on the edge of the bed.

*"Right, yer festering piece o' shit, what's the bassa's name agin?"* he said, semi slurring his words, the alcohol having had an immediate effect.

"B'stard." responded O'nad.

*"You might say Bastard, ya skinny, big eared heemasexual, ah say bassa, alright?"*

"No, you don't understand." began O'nad.

*"You callin' me thack?"* interjected McNad.

"No, no McNad, I was merely reiterating the name of the one we seek, for his name is B'stard, Dirty Terrence B'stard."

McNad sighed; disappointed that he was not going to have a violent conclusion to this conversation, his first in over two hundred years.

*"Fair enough"* he said *"So yer wantin' te know the whereaboots of this B'stard fella are ye?"*

"That's right." said O'nad.

*"Well, gi us a manut!"* McNad sat perfectly still on the bed, eyes closed momentarily, mouth agape. After a short while he reopened his eyes, a look of shock and revulsion clearly etched on the face-like features of this left testicle. At that precise moment he slowly raised his left leg and expelled the tiniest squeak of wind; its smallness not matched by the foul aroma that proceeded to permeate the previously clean air of the small room. O'nad covered his mouth and nose with his hand to shut out the vile, putrescent stench now emanating from this small Scottish testicle, the action had little effect and he had to stop himself from physically retching. McNad then closed his eyes again and inhaled deeply, relishing the beauty of his own wind.

*"Ah, it's all becoming clearer noo!"* he said, *"Ah can see 'im,…… he's bin sick on a bag fat burd,…….. oh, fer Christ's sakes she's fuckin' hideous!"* he ejaculated. O'nad passed him a tissue.

*"Reet, he's in a place known as The Dossers Arms Hotel,…….. it's a fuckin' dump, and it's aboot five miles from here!"* with that he let out another sigh and his arms, legs, face and epidydimal hair vanished. McNad had served his purpose and given O'nad what he had asked for. O'nad picked up the whisky sodden testicle and returned it to his jacket pocket. Slipping out of

the red shoes once more he sprayed some deodorant around the room.

# Chapter 15
## *"Missed Opportunity"*

By the time O'nad had woken the rest of the crew it was well past 7am. He'd waited a short while so that they could at least get some sleep, and he had hoped that B'stard had done the same. Unfortunately he had not.

The sleepy crew assembled in the reception of the comfortable hotel and sat waiting for O'nad to appear. Heinny had an uneasy feeling; perhaps, he thought, B'stard had made his wishes already and O'nad was about to warn them to escape before any harm could come to them. David was simply hoping that O'nad would tell them they could all go home, that this whole farce was over. Julia was sleepily staring at the patched up groin of her baboon friend. O'nad appeared in the foyer, having been outside to summon his cart.

"Come on everyone, quickly!" he shouted; everyone stood, as if to attention, in response to the command of O'nad, and made their way slowly towards the door. No one spoke. Once outside they boarded the cart and O'nad, once more, whipped his nag into action.

"I have been given some news." he announced to the expectant gang. Heinny thought the worst. "I have discovered the whereabouts of B'stard and, apparently, he's not feeling too clever at the moment." said O'nad, "So I'm hoping that this indicates that he's not yet had chance to recite any incantations and is sleeping off his illness in his hotel room." he went on;

"So who gave you this news?" asked Heinny.

"Your left testicle, Mr Himmler!" announced O'nad and explained how he had summoned the orienteering properties of the testicle – he didn't mention the appearance of McNad thinking that that little snippet of information was taking the tale a bit too far. Without expanding further O'nad continued to drive his horse onto the main arterial road which circled the town. David sat, silently worrying.

Once they had joined the A689 road into the centre of Hartlepool, O'nad set out his thoughts to the rest of the crew, the same thoughts he had imparted to Heinny a few hours earlier of how he hoped the situation would pan out. Everyone seemed to agree with O'nad, either that or they were all far too tired to argue. No matter how hard he tried to be positive, Heinny couldn't help the growing feeling that something wasn't going to go quite within O'nad's expectations.

It was another forty five minutes before they pulled up outside of The Dosser's Arms Hotell, some five miles from their own hotel. The fact that they had suffered the cart equivalent of a flat tyre (A snapped spoke – which O'nad had quickly repaired) did nothing to aid their progress. All seemed dumbstruck by the sheer deprivation the hotel exuded. The building itself was of smart Victorian construction, but the sandstone façade had been allowed to deteriorate to the point where only a full sandblasting would take away the years of filth and decay; the few windows which still contained panes of glass had not been shown a chamois leather for quite some considerable time and the ones where the glass had been broken were boarded up with cardboard, all of the frames were rotten, with flaking, yellowed paint. Above the shabby door a fading, hand painted sign read "The Dosser's Arms Hotell" the double 'l' in hotel served only to accentuate the downmarket image of the place.

O'nad held open the door to allow his friends to pass through into the uninviting interior, Heinny went in first, followed closely by Tobias, Julia and then David, all began to cough at the cloying, sickening, acrid stench of stale urine and vomit which hit their nostrils as soon as they entered the filthy building. The interior had obviously had a little bit of 'touching up' over the years for the reception desk was quite modern with a plush, but faded and stained, red dralon frontage. Behind it sat the most hideous harridan Heinny had ever seen; he swore he could see bits of carrot and tomato skin in her hair and this was confirmed when he reached the desk. She hadn't looked up from her copy of the Hartlepool Mail as they walked in and again, Heinny discovered why when he got to the reception, the lady, for that is what he assumed it to be from the length of her ginger hair, was sound asleep and snoring quite proficiently.

"Ahem!" he coughed as the others joined him; "Ahem!" louder this time and followed up with "Excuse me, Miss?" The 'Lady' stirred and let out an enormous fart, though the noise could have been made by her gigantic arms as they moved from her sides and onto the desk. In the same movement she brought her head up from her enormous bosom and one of her eyelids opened. She yawned loudly, revealing her four caries-ridden teeth and the exhalation brought forth a gust of the most vile, corrupt air which David thought he could actually taste for hours after the event. Even O'nad, who was still some twenty feet away in the doorway, was sickened by the foul blast, but in a perverse way was pleased with it as it took away the cloying urine smell.

"Huh!" she muttered "What the fuckin' 'ell a youse doin' in 'ere? Gerrout before ah call the cops!" she made for the telephone;

"No, wait!" said Heinny, "We're looking for a Dirty B'stard."

"Aren't we all mate? Nice outfit by the way." she sniggered.

"No, a Mister Dirty Terrence B'stard, and we have reason to believe he is staying here?"

"Oh, you mean our Terry, yeah he's been stayin' 'ere, but you've just missed 'im." she responded;

"You don't happen to know where he was heading do you?" asked O'nad as he approached the reception;

"Who wants to know, like and, er, what's it worth?" she asked.

"We're friends of his, and we've travelled up from London to help him celebrate his birthday, so if you could just let us know where he is now we'll get out of your hair." said O'nad;

"Well the crafty fucka, he never mentioned owt to me about it bein' 'is birthday, wait 'til ah see 'im!" she paused as if waiting for someone else to
speak, Heinny helped out.

"So, where is he then?" he asked again.

"Oh, 'e's been nicked for duffin' up this yella peril, like, carted off to nick about half an hour ago, good on 'im ah say, fuckin' traffic wardens, I 'ope 'e killed the cu.."

"Thank you Miss, that's quite enough information for now, do you know which station he's been taken to?" asked O'nad.

"'ow many d'ya think we've got like? 'artlepool, like!" she answered in the most courteous way she could. Everyone, except Maureen, turned tail and left the building as quickly as they could; not to race to the police station holding B'stard, but to escape the corrupt stench which emanated from the flabby, sweating arse of Maureen as she stood to point them in the right direction to said station.

"Well fuck ya's all then!" she tutted, "Some people 'ave no manners!"
She checked her watch, after pulling back the several folds of flab on her lower arm and wiping away some semi-dried vomit from its face, and saw that it was 8 am. Her shift was over. She retired to her room within the building, the room that came with the job.

O'nad, Heinny, Tobias and the Snaiths re-boarded their cart and made haste for Hartlepool Police station to try to catch B'stard being released. What they heard when they got there made them jump for joy.

"I'm sorry, but he won't be going anywhere today." said the officer on front desk. "To be honest, I wouldn't be surprised if the magistrate doesn't throw away the key on him, he's nearly killed one of our best traffic wardens. He'll certainly be remanded, that I can guarantee." What he didn't tell them was that his brother was the magistrate.

On leaving the police station the crew found a nearby café to sit and ponder their next move. It was obvious that B'stard would be out of action for some time if what the officer had told them was proved correct. O'nad could not contain his joy at this news and sat smiling inanely to himself whilst Julia ordered the drinks.

"What luck!" he said to Tobias;

"Luck indeed," replied his skeletal friend, "But what of his possessions? The book and, most importantly, our baboon friend's genitalia, where are they now?"

O'nad pondered the question for a while and was about to answer when David interrupted;

"They'll have taken them off him, surely, and even if they haven't he won't be able to do much with them whilst he's inside, will he?" he half asked, half stated.

"I suppose not." replied O'nad, not convinced by his own answer. He hoped that they'd taken them from him and that they were languishing, in much the same way as B'stard himself, in a secure store, but he had an uneasy feeling that they had not.

## Chapter 16
*"No Blacks Please"*

Anul Abu-Sar was freed from imprisonment the day after his confrontation with B'stard, the parole board believing that he no longer posed a significant threat to the public, having only been caught once in the five years of his sentence, buggering a fellow inmate – on that occasion they had given him the benefit of the doubt as at the time of the alleged offence he had been sharing a cell with Michael Carrymore, the well known TV games show host, who had recently been 'outed' by the press, and was in prison following an unfortunate incident at the swimming baths; and so Anul was released, though on licence, to serve the rest of his sentence within the community.

B'stard had thought of utilising the powers of his cloak of invisibility to escape from his cell but thought better of it deciding, instead, to serve his full sentence and be freed legitimately rather than become a fugitive. He was released some two and a half hours after Anul and the pair met up, as they had arranged, in the salubrious surroundings of The Dosser's Arms Hotell (with two 'l's').

Anul arrived first and sat, waiting patiently, for his new employer, in the less than plush dining room of the derelict hotel. They had been due to meet at 10am and Anul had arrived in good time at 09:55, he was not concerned that the time on his wristwatch was now showing 10:10, rather he sat patiently flicking through the pages of a well thumbed copy of 'Asian Boys'. He did not notice the odd, buttock shaped indentations in the seat opposite him, nor did he hear the feint breathing as B'stard sat, watching his new found ally.

B'stard was just about to break the silence and reveal his presence when he observed a change in Anul's demeanour. Anul had gone from being rather composed and patient, as he awaited the arrival of his Lord and Master, to a state of nervous, tense agitation. B'stard was curious as to what was causing this change in his friend's behaviour and so decided to maintain his cloak of invisibility for a few moments more. It all became much clearer to B'stard as the seconds began to unfold. Anul's breathing became more laboured as he continued to flick the pages of his 'Art Pamphlet'; he gazed around, as if to calibrate his surroundings, in a way that suggested that his next move would be one of a covert nature. *"What could be so secretive that would cause Anul to lose so much composure?"* thought B'stard. It didn't take long before Anul's intentions were made clear.

The less than plush surroundings of the Dining Room which was occupied, seemingly singularly by Anul, were dimly lit. The room itself was situated along an equally dimly lit corridor that led from the reception area. Anul had carefully observed that all was quiet in the room and indeed the immediate vicinity. The hotel was never a bustling hive of activity, due in the main to the 'down-market' raison de'tre of the facility in question. Today, however, was an extremely quite day, even for the Dosser's Arms. The hotel was so quiet that Anul could quite easily be convinced that he was the only occupant. B'stard looked on with anticipation and bated breath.

Anul became more agitated and began to writhe about on his seat. His writhing turned to riling and alternated back and forth in a way that suggested that he might have been suffering from the presence of threadworm. Anyone who has ever had, or known anyone to have had, threadworm will know that this peculiar motion is a tried and trusted way to facilitate relief from the rectal

# A Crofter's Tale (The REAL Story of The Hartlepool Monkey)

itching brought on as a symptom of the aforementioned, parasitic, infection. Should this form of 'hands-free' scratching not satiate the relief of itching then the next course of action would normally be the insertion of a digit (from either hand though in the case of Anul, being a Sikh, it would likely be his left hand) into the offending orifice, followed by a vigorous scraping. Following this remedial course of action the affected person would then, although lots of sufferers would usually deny the next step, remove their digit and proceed to run it under their nasal passageway as if to take in the delicate bouquet of sweat, bum-fluff and faecal matter – such is the fascination, with most people, of all things relating to shit. There's a copraphile in every one of us, though physiological growth research normally suggests that the 'Anal Stage' is outgrown after about 2-3 years of age.

Anyway, as far as B'stard could make out, everything appeared to suggest that his Asian friend was the unfortunate host of a parasitic, worm-like intruder. Not only was Anul continuing to shift his lower body more energetically upon his chair, he had observed that Anul was now proceeding to loosen the belt from his trousers. *"This is it!"* though B'stard. *"He's going to scratch his brown-eye. There must be a sailor thinking about him!"* he laughed to himself; *"I'll at least afford him the opportunity to end his discomfort before revealing myself, but my timing has to be just right otherwise I'll have to bear witness to him sniffing at his pooh stained fingers, and I've just had my breakfast".*

Anul, after further loosening his belt then began to unzip his flies. It was all too obvious for B'stard now as he awaited the inevitable intervention. However, at this point things started to go slightly differently. For although Anul had loosened his belt and unzipped his flies he then proceeded to slowly get up from his stool (that is to say, his seat and not a faecal discharge) and slowly slide his trousers down to his knees. *"Perhaps he is looking to position himself to as to get extra purchase?"* thought B'stard. This wasn't the case. Anul then plunged his hand into his beige yfronts (with chocolate brown piping). The difference being that Anul had plunged his hand into the front of his under-garments, rather than the back (as B'stard had originally expected – based on his 'threadworm' theory). It then all became only too clear. Not only was Anul crouched (in a hunched way) over, almost double, he had carefully placed his 'Art Pamphlet' on the seat of his chair so as to make reference to the pages within as he started to make rhythmic gestures in it's direction. These rhythmic gestures were also accompanied by a set of familiar grunts and groans. *"Oh my God!"* thought B'stard. *"He hasn't got worms at all. The filthy swine's knocking one off."*

B'stard was now in a bit of a dilemma. Should he expose himself (that is to say make himself visible to Anul rather than commit a lewd act) or wait until the Sikh was finished. He pondered the pros and cons of each horn of his dichotomy very quickly. If he did choose to reveal himself then surely Anul would ask how long he had been there which would, no doubt, lead the Sikh to accuse B'stard of voyeuristic intent. He dared not risk this allegation for he wanted to maintain some level of credibility when he set about conquering the world. After all, it wouldn't go down too well with his subjects if they knew anything of his indiscretions; and so B'stard decided that he would wait until his friend was finished 'bashing his bishop' (or other relevant Sikh related religious hierarchical euphemism).

After a few frantic tugs Anuls Herculean task was complete. It is well documented that Hercules himself had ten labours to carry out for the Gods, each of which was intended to stretch the Hero to breaking point and designed to ensure certain failure. Although Anul only had this one task to complete, he did so in a fashion that would have impressed the mighty Zeus himself. When he had finished his onerous task he let go a mighty sigh of relief which was accompanied by a release of 'man-fat' or 'liquid-lard'. The sight of this caused B'stard's stomach to turn over. He would surely be reunited with his breakfast if he didn't remove himself from the offending arena of self abuse. B'stard, slowly and quietly got to his feet, all the time maintaining his view of Anul, for fear that his friend may detect his presence. B'stard headed for the toilet facilities of the hotel which were situated just outside of the dining room (but any patron could be forgiven for mistaking any part of this establishment as a place of convenience). Just before he left the dining room and Anul to himself B'stard turned to see his friend wipe the remnants of seminal fluid across the sleeves of his tunic like garment. This was enough to set B'stard off as he set off for the lavatories *"Heughh!..... Bleurghh!"*

Once inside the toilets B'stard emptied the contents of his stomach, bade farewell to his breakfast (which had been with him for only 30 minutes or so) and freshened up (as best as any patron of the Dosser's Arms could) using the solitary miniscule bar, nay, nugget of dried soap present in the grubby, lime scale covered basin. *"He must surely be finished now!"* he thought to himself and made for the door and indeed the dining room (where he had since vowed never to consume another morsel).

As B'stard was about to enter the dining room he realised he was still invisible. Fearing that continuing to remain in such a condition might bring about a new set of unwelcome events, he quickly turned over his palms, shuffled his hands back and forth and whispered "Just like that"; in an instant he was visible again just as he rounded the corner and entered the room occupied by Anul.

"Ah, Anul, I see that you've made it! I trust your journey to these here premises was a stress free one and that it didn't take too much out of you?" he added. Anul, still breathless from his recent exertions, responded

"Yes, I made it alright, what a relief.... Phew..... I must apologise for me being somewhat out of breath, only I had to run in order to catch the bus this morning." he went on to add.

"You lying creep" B'stard whispered.

"Sorry, what did you say?" asked Anul.

"Oh, nothing my friend, it's good to see you once more." B'stard lied. Anul offered up his hand so as to reciprocate B'stard's pleasure of seeing him once more. The hand that was offered up for the 'hand-shake' gesture was the very hand which had been utilised for a very different kind of 'shake' moments before, and as such had been coated with the Sikh's seminal fluid only 5 minutes since. B'stard, wishing not to offend the Sikh, but equally not wanting to oblige in the traditional welcoming gesture instead curtseyed in a curiously feminine way. Anul was obviously taken aback with this response and gazed back at B'stard inquisitively. B'stard then replied

Oh, I'm from the south, its just the way we do things down there!" Anul thought nothing of this and proceeded to take a seat opposite B'stard.

"Now for some business Mr Abu-Sar" stated B'stard.

"Indeed" offered the Sikh. "Where and what now?" he added.

"All in good time my friend, all in good time" responded B'stard. "First I need to go through some biographic details with you"

"Some what?" asked Anul.

"Listen, I know I intimated that I would offer you a place as second in command, by my side in my quest for universal glory, but I cannot offer you this 'place' officially without going through the correct procedures"

"What procedures" retorted Anul.

"Your job interview, that's what" asserted B'stard.

"Oh, well if you must, only I wished you'd told me sooner, it's just that I haven't prepared" said Anul nervously.

"Not to worry Mr Abu-Sar, this is an informal interview, one from which you can expect my decision as soon as it is complete" added B'stard.

"Fire away then, Mr B'stard".

# A Crofter's Tale (The REAL Story of The Hartlepool Monkey)

## *The Interview:*

In order not to get bogged down in B'stard's interview techniques and protocol we can assume that items such as name, date of birth and nationality have already been covered and as such we will join the interview at a more pertinent juncture.

"Mr Abu-Sar, you say you are keen on taking on the position of Second in Command, specifically of my Army of the Dead, and assisting me in taking over the world as part of my megalomaniacal plans for overall universal domination, but tell me what experience do you have in this field?"

Anul paused for a moment. He had never been asked such a question and even if he had it would probably never have been asked in this way!

"Well, erm, I don't. That is to say I've never been given the opportunity. But that doesn't mean to say I'm not keen…!" he replied.

"Hmm," gestured B'stard. "No, specific, experience." he muttered as he jotted down the response in his notebook. "What experience do you have then that is of an evil and heinous nature?"

"Oh, I've got loads of that Mr B'stard, remember I told you all this in the prison cell only the other day."

"You misunderstand Anul I mean evil and heinous, not evil and anus!" condescended B'stard.

"Well, other than my crimes of grand necromancy and grievous buggery I once, whilst running my convenience store, altered the calibration of the food scales so as to misrepresent the weight of goods (in my favour). The extent of this misrepresentation amounted to customer fraud, the act of which saw my gross profits rise by more than 12% without any efforts or additional capital input." explained Anul.

"Quite interesting Mr Abu-Sar, fraud is indeed a crime though I'm not sure it is evil or heinous enough to warrant the offering of the prestigious post that is available. Have you anything else to add?" asked B'stard.

# A Crofter's Tale (The REAL Story of The Hartlepool Monkey)

"Indeed I do Mr B'stard for whilst that in itself is not particularly evil I do recall almost being 'rumbled'"

"Really? Please, go on" asked B'stard.

"Well, I was serving a young boy, about 10 years old, with his usual quarter of a pound of Lion's Midget Gems. I remember the boy well as he would always ask for 'No Blacks', the racist swine. Anyway, because he regularly feasted upon the same comestibles, daily, he had the uncanny sense of being able to calibrate the contents weight by mere hand-related judgement. He confronted me one day when I'd used the erroneous scales to measure his requested weight related order. 'You've diddled me' said the boy as he jiggled the contents of the bag momentarily. 'And I estimate the extent of the diddling to be in the region of circa six [6] discrete candies'. I thought the game was up for surely this racist upstart would report me to the weights and measures people and I would receive a hefty fine for my unscrupulous dealings."

"What did you do next then Mr Abu-Sar?" asked B'stard.

"Well, not wanting to be reported to the authorities for crimes against the honest provision of groceries to the general public, I picked up the pick handle I had ensconced beneath my serving counter (which I used as 'reasonable' protection) and brought it crashing down on the youth's skull, killing him instantly. I did, however, make sure the child had paid for his sweets before carrying out the act."

"Bloody hell Anul that was a bit strong wasn't it?" asked B'stard.

"You better believe it Mr B'stard, it clear snapped my pick handle in two and they don't come cheap you know." replied Anul.

"It's not exactly what I meant Anul, but please do go on. What next?" "Well Mr B'stard, I put his body in the fridge, dismembered his cold corpse, minced his flesh and bones and sold the 'meat' to the local 'Ye Olde Pie Shoppe' as grade one fresh meat. I got £2:00 per pound for it, making me a total clear net profit of £120. Not bad eh!" added Anul.

"No not bad at all Mr Abu-Sar. I need a man who has an eye for detail, especially when it comes to monies and all things financial. The job's yours…!"

"Thank you Mr B'stard, I'll not let you down." said Anul. The two of them then shook hands in order to seal the deal. B'stard immediately wished he hadn't but too late was the cry.

"Let us celebrate our new found alliance Mr Abu-Sar with two pints of the finest local brew." offered B'stard.

Now given that the Dosser's Arms Hotell was based in Hartlepool the suggested means of celebrating would only be correct on two parts; firstly, they could procure two pints, and secondly the two pints in question would be local. However, as for being the 'finest' I would again remind the reader that our story takes place in Hartlepool.

"Two pints it is then Mr B'stard, allow me to buy these." said Anul. "All I need to do is attract the attention of the receptionist." he said.

"Shit!" replied B'stard. "If she sees me here, having a drink, she'll pester the living daylights out of me." he added and with that he shuffled his hands, palm down, back and forth and uttered the magical words *"Just like that!"* Anul watched, amazed then headed off to get the beers in.

Anul made his way to the reception area leaving his friend, B'stard, unseen in the dining room. Once at reception he rang the bell that he hoped would attract the attention of the member of staff on duty. He rang and rang and rang the bell until it came apart in his hands. Anul saw that the bell was of cheap make, being base metal plated with a brass effect, and of even poorer construction, so flimsy that it would take no more than a few hundred bangs before it disintegrated, leaving the unfortunate ringer with nothing more than the bell-end in his hand. This was not at all unusual for our friend.

Despite having rang persistently for what seemed like an age there was no response from the other side of the reception counter. However, a strange and acrid smell started to emanate from the aforementioned general direction. The smell was so obscene that it caused Anul to check the contents of his pants for fear that he may have inadvertently, and quite by accident, shit himself. Only when he checked that he had not, indeed, dirtied his pants did he realise where the stench was coming from. It was coming from Maureen.

"What the fuck's goin' on 'ere, who d'ya think yer are, fucking Quasi-fucking-modo what with all that bastard bell ringing?" bellowed Maureen. Anul, reeled and cowered for a moment, in the main as a reaction to the foul smell which enveloped him, doing so only served to further accentuate the hunch on his back.

"Er, sorry love, didn't see you there. I thought it was them bloody kids again pissing around with me bell, no offence intended love." replied Maureen both sheepishly and apologetically. These were new traits for Maureen. She'd heard about them during her training but dismissed them as myth or that only a stuck up bastard would behave in this way. She was wrong, but at least she was learning, and to Maureen it felt both strange and satisfying. Not wanting to let the 'new' moment go Maureen went on to ask "Well, what the fuck do you want? Er, I mean, what the fuck do you want sir, please, thank you, begging your pardon……….. Oh, fuck it…… what do ya want you hunchbacked freak!" asked, nay, demanded Maureen as she immediately reverted back to type.

"Two pints of ale please, and can you serve them in the dining room?" asked Anul.

"Yeh, suppose. Stick a fucking broom up me arse and a'll sweep the bastard floor whilst I'm at it!" said Maureen.

"I'll take that as a yes then shall I?" asked Anul.

"Yes." tutted Maureen.

After only 2 short hours the drinks were served to the patiently awaiting Anul and his 'missing' guest!

"Friend not turned up?" asked Maureen nosily, and continued "Or are you just a greedy get?" she tittered to herself.

"No, I'm expecting a friend at any time." replied Anul. Maureen left Anul to his drinks, turning tail only once to remove a dampened receipt from the cavernous crevice of her cleavage; she banged it on the table next to the drinks; it totalled £12.80 plus a service charge of £2.50, and the handwritten bill 'reminded' patrons that "gratuities" were **not** included.

Not wishing to tempt fate B'stard chose to remain invisible throughout his ensuing conversation with Anul. Another meeting with Maureen was more than his patience or stomach could take.

"So Mr B'stard what plans have you devised regarding world domination and pray, tell me more of the Army of the Dead!" asked Anul earnestly.

"Well Mr Abu-Sar the plan is quite simple and goes thus................"

# Chapter 17
## *"The Chance Encounter"*

O'nad, Heinny, Tobias, David & Julia sat and pondered their next move. Silence was predominant as they all sat in the Café in which they had assembled. Several minutes passed, as did several double espressos and cappuccinos. The waitress of the "Greasy Spoon" café was indeed extremely busy that day. Julia piped up;

"Any one for some light refreshment? The sight of all these caffeine based imbibements passing by for the benefit of other customers is making me thirsty and I could well do with something that would slake the aforementioned thirst".

"Have you swallowed a fucking dictionary?" asked David, as the rest of our friends looked on in amazement at Julia's seemingly perfect grasp of the English language spoken.

"Well, what I'm **trying** to say is that I could do with a drink, after all we have been here for some time and the waitress is looking at us in a funny way." responded Julia.

"Trying?" snapped David. "Oh, you're trying alright. Have you stopped to think that she may be looking at us in a 'funny way' because of the five of us sitting here one of us.. (pointing to Heinny) .. is a monkey, a talking one at that, whilst another.. (pointing at Tobias)… is recently resurrected from a 200 year grave and stinks to the high heavens, whilst this one… (pointing to O'Nad).. is just plain odd. Tell me Julia, could this be the real reason she is looking at us in a 'funny way' or is the waitress simply genuinely concerned that we haven't placed a fucking order yet?....... you stupid bitch!"

Now we all know that David can be quite cutting in his remarks to Julia.

We know that he certainly excels in both sarcasm and condescension but this time he'd gone too far. Julia started to sob uncontrollably. She reached for one of the expertly folded paper napkins to wipe the tears from her dewy eyes, looked at David and simply said "Bastard!"

"Where?" asked Tobias.

"Pardon" said Julia.

"Where's B'stard? Is he here?"

"No Tobias, you misunderstand. David's the bastard." she explained. "So" said Tobias. "We have in our midst a double agent. How did you reveal his identity?" The others looked on aghast at what Tobias was saying, scarcely believing that their friend could be so stupid as to take, quite literally, what Julia was saying about her husband.

# A Crofter's Tale (The REAL Story of The Hartlepool Monkey)

"You thick sod Toby!" said O'Nad. "Julia was, is, referring to David, her husband, who is a bastard by nature and not, I repeat not, by name. It is the latter who we seek and not our erstwhile friend Mr Snaith. Mr Snaith's only crime is that he is an insensitive chauvinistic pig of the highest order. Quite what Julia sees in him beggars belief."

"Ah, I see" said Tobias. "Sorry about that. It's just that I'm a bit slow on the neuro-linguistic front presently. You must understand I've not used my brain in more than 200 years so I'm a little out of practise." explained Tobias.

"That's okay Tobias." said Julia. "David hasn't used his brain since he was born." she sniped as she gave her husband the most frightful glower that had ever been, well, glowered.

Still sobbing Julia got up and made for the wash room. Heinny sensed Julia's obvious distress and followed her.

"Julia's right. We could all do with something to drink and something to eat. What's everyone having?" asked O'Nad.

Now, without going into too much detail (for fear of extending the length of this chapter unnecessarily) we can assume our friends chose their preferred refreshments and that the waitress had obliged them by bringing said requested items to their table. However, for those of a curious nature, the following is the definitive list of items ordered:

O'Nad – 1 x cup of English Tea (75p) plus 1 x wholemeal scone (65p) = £1.40
Tobias – 1 x cup of Hot Chocolate (80p) plus 1 x slice of hot buttered toast (40p) = £1.20.
David – 1 x glass of fresh orange (95p) plus 1 x blueberry muffin (80p) = £1.75
Heinny – 1 x cup of cappuccino (£1.00) plus 1 x bunch of banana's (£2.40p) = £3.40.

A Crofter's Tale (The REAL Story of The Hartlepool Monkey)

Julia – 1 x cup of herbal tea – camomile (75p) plus 1 x strawberry yoghurt (50p) = £1.35.
Total Amount Payable = £9.10 pence
Total paid = £10.00 (tip included of 90p).

Meanwhile, in the washroom Julia stood looking at her image reflected in the mirror positioned just above the basin. She carefully wiped the tears from her eyes so as not to compromise the heavily applied mascara which she'd 'plastered on' just a few hours earlier. Her attempts to do so were, however, in vain as with every wipe the eye make-up simply spread and spread until all at once it looked, for a moment, that the reflection staring back was that of a Panda (though if the truth were to be known the resemblance was more akin to that of aged rocker Alice Cooper). This did not help Julia and she continued to let gush tears of unhappiness and distress. She decided to cease her futile attempt at drying her eyes and instead turned her attentions to her mouth which, by now, was a blubbering mass of spittle. She carefully mopped at her salivating orifice only to discover, to her continued horror that her lipstick had smeared also. Looking at her reflection once more it now seemed that Alice Cooper had vanished, only to be replaced with Robert Smith (formerly of The Cure). She was a single step away from looking a complete and utter clown and if she had persisted in her attempts to smarten herself up then she would have indeed looked smart; that of Billy Smart (famous character in the field of clownery and all things relating to clowneries).

"There, there Julia." came a friendly and familiar voice. It was that of Heinny, who had followed her into the washroom. Julia instinctively turned to face her beloved simian. It was at this point that both Julia's and Heinny's emotions changed. Looking upon Robert, erm, I mean Julia Heinny gazed at the true beauty that stood before him. Normally, modern conventions would dictate that such a sight, offered up to the male of the species (the species in question being human) would be met with a combination of extreme revulsion and howls of derisive laughter. However, Heinny was neither human nor conventional. To him, the sight that stood before him was that of consummate beauty and perfection personified. Julia sensed that Heinny was becoming aroused (quite how with the absence of testosterone which is manufactured in the gonads, of which Heinny had none, remains an enigma but aroused he was) and flung her arms around the excited monkey. Heinny reciprocated and flung his arms, in a gibbon like fashion, around Julia.

"Oh, Heinny my love, my dear, dear Baboon. Hold me in your strong and excessively long arms." Heinny did as Julia asked, and more to boot. His arms and hands caressed every inch of Julia's body but in the main her buttocks and her small, bee sting like, breasts. Through his sensitive mauling of Julia's body he could perceive that one buttock was bigger (by almost 50%) than the other and even stranger this 'imbalance' spread to her breasts as one of those (the left one) was bigger than its opposing partner. These traits are commonplace in the Baboon fraternity, especially Heinny's Flange, and as such this further stirred Heinny's emotions which, in turn, stirred his manhood which stood to attention at a whopping nine centimetres. This was almost double the size and girth that Julia was used to with her husband, David.

A tide of emotion and passion swept the pair off their feet and all at once they found themselves behind the locked door of one of the cubicles within the washroom. The rest must now, for the sake of common decency, and so as not to infringe bestiality laws, be left to imagination save to say that Julia got a good old fashioned seeing to. Seconds later the pair emerged; Julia composed herself and began to re-dress. Heinny did nothing as he was spent. Instead he observed his loved one as she hoisted her over-sized buttock into the gusset of her knickers. Julia observed that Heinny was watching and she gave him a sly wink of the eye. Before long, and after she had secured her oddly paired breasts back within the hammock from whence they first came, the love struck duo were ready to emerge from their forbidden abode. The memories of that first liaison would, forever, be etched in the memory of Julia along with the scratch marks now visible on her buttocks left by her passionate lover.

O'nad, Tobias and David were just finishing their snacks as the two re-emerged at the table of the café.

"Sorry Julia." proclaimed David in an apologetic tone.

"Forget it David, I have!" she responded whilst simultaneously giving Heinny a sly nudge. This nudge was followed by a wink and the process was further repeated (in the age old traditions of a typical 'nudge, nudge, wink, wink style).

Once they had all reassembled, they finished the last remnants of their repast and Julia took out, from her handbag, a pipe which she duly stuffed with tobacco and lit with a series of determined sucks. Again, she looked at Heinny as she did this and, did it in a way that was overtly sexual, even to our otherwise oblivious heroes. Heinny reciprocated by making a 'ring-like' shape with the forefinger and thumb of his left hand and, pushing the index finger of his right hand in and out of the newly formed ring, mouthed the words *"You filthy slut, you want it don't you?"* Julia giggled as he made this rude gesture. This caused David to look at Heinny. Heinny had seemingly been caught in the act as David observed the strange actions being carried out by the Baboon.

"What are you doing Heinny?" asked David. Caught somewhat off guard, and more than slightly embarrassed, Heinny responded "Oh, it's nothing David, I've just got an itch on my thumb which I'm trying to scratch." Gullible as he was, and is, David thought nothing of this and went about draining the last remnants of his orange juice. Heinny and Julie realised they had both had a close shave, Julia's being closer as Heinny was still immensely hirsute, and decided to curtail their love-struck shenanigans to a later time.

"Hey, you guys! I've just had a thought" proclaimed Tobias.

"Careful now Toby you know your brain isn't fully operational yet" said O'nad.

"No, seriously listen. We assume, don't we, that the journal and the sac are either in the hands of B'stard or that they are in the hands of the prison authorities?"

"Yes I suppose we do." replied Heinny.

"Well, given that B'stard probably didn't intend to get arrested on the morning he beat up the Traffic Warden there may well be a possibility that the journal and sac are somewhere else!"

"Where might that be Tobias?" asked David.

"The Dosser's Arms, in the room where he has been staying. He may, just may, have kept it there for safe keeping"

"Brilliant!" said O'nad. "If that is the case then it may be possible to retrieve them before B'stard gets out of prison." he added. "Whoopee" announced Heinny "I'm going to be reunited with my full compliment genitalia!" he further whooped.

"Hmmm" gesticulated Julia, as she licked her lips in wanton excitement.

"Holy testiculations!" announced O'nad. "There's not a moment to lose. Quick to the Horse-cart!" he announced further (in the style of Adam West – Batman c1966-1968).

With that our heroes got up and rushed to the door of the Greasy Spoon Café. Within seconds, well minutes, well actually more like 15 minutes, they were aboard their trusty chariot heading at break neck speed (if you happen to be a three-toed sloth) for the Dosser's Arms Hotell (2 x Ls).

## Chapter 18
*"Another Chance Encounter"*

In the time it took for O'nad's crew to discover that their foe had been incarcerated 'at Her Majesty's Pleasure', Anul Abu-Sar had been released from prison; in the time it took for them to gather at the Greasy Spoon café, and discuss the potential whereabouts of the Journal and it's accompanying sac, true British Justice had been served and Dirty Terrence B'stard had also been released into the community. It would seem that 'Her Majesty's Pleasure' is significantly shorter these days – which is understandable given that Phillip and her are both in their eighties; and so a violent, power obsessed animal and a hunchbacked pervert were freed into society and both made their way to The Dosser's Arms Hotell.('L' to the power of 2)

O'nad's crew arrived some three hours later, their mode of transport being what it was, combined with the evening rush hour traffic through central Hartlepool (Two Morris Minors, both of which seemed to have broken down, and a trolleybus), just as Anul and B'stard – though from appearance it would have seemed as if it was simply Anul – were beginning to discuss the way forward; and just as Maureen was beginning her final sixteen hour night shift.

On arriving at work Maureen had proudly announced that she had been 'head hunted' by the YMCA Hostel further down the street, and that she would be on 5p an hour more than her current hourly rate.

Heinny approached the reception desk prepared, through previous experience, for the onslaught of putrescent odours about to be unleashed from the breath and body of the delightful Maureen. Inhaling deeply, almost to the point of hyperventilating, he gulped as much as he could of the less rank air of the hallway, into his lungs so that he might better cope with the filth he was about to breathe.

"Hello again." he said without breathing out, Maureen looked up without a flicker of recognition, staring blankly at the baboon standing before her; she belched audibly. Unperturbed Heinny continued, "You may recall we were looking for our friend Mister B'stard?" Nothing. "Er…. well we were wondering if we could ask a favour of you?" Maureen remained in a semi catatonic state as she replied "What?" Heinny went on, "I said would it be possible for us to hide in his room so that we might spring a surprise on him when he gets back from, er,..released, from prison, it being his birthday and all, please?" he turned his face away from her to inhale some more of the slightly fresher air, turning back just as she inhaled deeply and bellowed *"Ah don't fuckin' think so like!"* letting out a torrent of the foulest and most halitosis-ridden breath Heinny had ever been unfortunate enough to encounter. So bad was it that he immediately felt his stomach turn and he began to retch involuntarily, desperately trying his best to maintain his Greasy Spoon luncheon within the walls of his belly. He succeeded in keeping his food down only for as long as it took Maureen to utter her next sentence;

"Unless you wanna pay me, in kind, fotha pleasure, big boy, if you catch my meaning, eh?" at the same time she pouted in her most provocative manner whilst simultaneously pushing her ample and sweat soaked bosoms into the face of the unfortunate monkey. Heinny immediately let forth a torrent of vomit directly into Maureen's face, the powerful force of the flow sufficient to hold her mouth open; the vomit finding its way into her lungs and stomach as she battled to close her gaping, cavernous mouth, inhaling desperately, gasping for air yet drowning in baboon puke.

When Heinny had drained his stomach contents he stood watching, in astonished disbelief, as Maureen keeled over, apparently dead. He didn't feel the need to confirm this apparent sudden death; rather he hastily walked away from the scene and outside of the hotel to speak with his friends.

As the remaining members gathered on the steps leading up to the hotel doors a panicked Heinny came rushing out, his pallor reminiscent of a mortuary resident as opposed to a monkey, the others noticed that there was what looked to be vomit dripping from his chin and down his chest; Julia spoke first, concerned for her new lover,

"What happened to you?" she exclaimed.

Heinny relished the fresh air outside, breathing a great lung full of the stuff before answering his friends' concerns;

"It's hell in there!" he said. The others understood but were determined that they should all go back inside and try to recover the journal and sac. Heinny reluctantly agreed and once more began to hyperventilate to save his lungs from further damage by the toxic fumes within.

Our famous five approached the desk with caution just as one of the hotel kitchen staff was trying to resuscitate Maureen; the fact that he felt the need to cover her mouth and entire face with at least three towels to avoid the potential contamination was not lost on any of them. Sadly, the placing of the towels served only to restrict the amount of air he was able to pass into Maureen's lungs and she failed to respond after a number of attempts at mouth to mouth, or mouth to towel as was the case, the 'number' of attempts being precisely one. The paramedics, who arrived within hours, commended the kitchen worker on his efforts in the face of such aromatic adversity. They did not attempt to revive the corpulent teenager and duly pronounced her dead at the scene, affirming that death was as a result of choking on her own vomit after excessive consumption of banana. Heinny looked away guiltily. A post mortem on the unfortunate Maureen would later confirm that she did indeed drown on her own vomit but that she had consumed up to twelve Cornish Pasties and about a litre and a half of Diet Coke, curiously, there would be no trace of her ever having eaten a banana that day. Maureen's dreams of working at the YMCA Hostel had been cruelly dashed. The YMCA's dreams of recruiting a highly experienced, forward thinking and professional, receptionist were also laid to rest.

Once their nasal passages had accustomed themselves to the fetid air in the hotel, O'nad approached the new receptionist to enquire about B'stard's room number; he was closely followed by Tobias Wat.

"Can I ask what it's in connection with, Sir?" enquired the replacement for Maureen.

"Well, it's a rather delicate matter." he said, quickly flashing his St John Ambulance First Aider certificate, in a manner which would indicate that he wanted the receptionist to believe that he was an officer of the law.

"You will be aware that Mr B'stard was arrested for a serious assault a few days ago?" the receptionist nodded affirmatively, "Well, myself and my colleague here need to have access to his room to determine if other offences have been committed; offences of a more serious nature; how can I say this? We believe that he may have images secreted about his belongings; images of an offensive nature, images so vile, corrupt and perverse that they sicken even the strongest stomach, so disgusting in their nature that, in the wrong hands, they could twist immature minds, do you understand me?" the receptionist understood fully and duly issued the 'officers' with a duplicate key to room 17.

O'nad thanked the receptionist and turned to gather the rest of his team together only to find that they were standing just outside of what looked to be the eating area of the hotel, passing sniggers, chuckles and titters between them. Curious as to what it was that they found so amusing, O'nad hurried across the foyer to join them. The doorway was blocked by the ample frame of Heinny as well as the uneven and equally ample body of Julia,

David was standing just inside the room, O'nad had to jump up so that he could see over the five foot six baboon's shoulder; within the otherwise vacant dining room he could see a hunchbacked Sikh chattering away to himself and drinking beer, apparently to excess – for he had two 'lined up' in front of him.

"He's actually having a full conversation with himself!" exclaimed Julia giggling like a schoolgirl and pushing the larger of her two buttocks into the throbbing groin of Heinny who stood behind her. David stood to her left, obviously oblivious to the obvious grinding between the monkey and his wife. All three tittered and sniggered in a most childish way.

"It's very clever the way he answers himself in a different voice though, don't you think?" the others listened intently, "It's like he's a ventriloquist or something!" said Julia, David tutted loudly before sarcastically quoting his unfortunate wife in a mocking manner,

"'It's like he's a ventriloquist or something' stupid bitch! You mean he IS a ventriloquist!" O'nad immediately sought to calm the situation and interrupted the bickering pair by holding aloft the key to B'stard's room.

"I have the key to B'stard's room!" he said quietly, Heinny was extremely pleased and excited, the latter being apparent, quite obviously, to all who cared to cast an eye upon his groin, though the baboon's reasons for pleasure and excitement were entirely different.

"Let's go and search his room for the book, and Mr Himmler's sac." continued O'nad, ending this little conversational treat with "Can't you do something to hide that, Heinny?" Heinny shrugged his shoulders, "I'm a monkey, what do you expect?" he said and the gang set forth in search of B'stard's room.

Tobias was distracted momentarily by the loud guffaw that emanated from within the dining room. He turned towards the door as the others began to climb the stairs. What Wat heard set the hairs on his neck to full attention and sent a shiver down his spine.

# A Crofter's Tale (The REAL Story of The Hartlepool Monkey)

"So once I have a need I will simply summon the army to my command and set the wheels in motion for world domination." said the hunchback, though in the 'other' voice. Tobias didn't see his lips move once, not even a cheek muscle twitched to indicate that this hunched individual was in any way adept in the art of ventriloquism. His concern grew when he then heard the Sikh utter

"You're sure they're all dead, this army of yours, Master?"

"As far as I can gather, from what the journal tells me, they are all very dead, yes. Why the sudden interest in them being dead?" came the second voice again, Tobias immediately recognised the dulcet tones of the one who had resurrected him and the one who had dealt him the cruellest blow by usurping his claim to the wishes. The hunchbacked Sikh was somehow having a conversation with Mister Dirty B'stard; but how? There was clearly nobody in the chair opposite the hunchback; Tobias was sure that the voice wasn't coming from the same person, as the Sikh clearly had a completely different tone of voice and his accent was obviously Indian in origin. He listened again though more surreptitiously, concealing himself behind a large, but clearly dead, aspidistra plant.

"So, as I was saying," continued the voice he now knew to be B'stard, "When the time comes to summon the army, I will simply command them to follow your orders, they will have no option but to obey, and your orders from me are to infiltrate the very parts of the political make up of this great country of ours, so as to further my interests and get me the ears of those necessary for me to gain the political upper hand as a first step to my megalomaniacal plans!"

Without listening further Tobias turned and ran for the stairs to find his missing friends. He found O'nad, David, Julia and Heinny on the second floor, all were holding handkerchiefs over their mouths and noses for the stench in this part of the building was far worse than anything they had come across downstairs; they were standing silently outside of room 17, whispering so as not to disturb the occupant. Tobias approached them purposefully.

"Found you at last!" he shouted.

His four friends turned and each put a finger to their own lips in a 'shushing' manner.

"Oh don't worry about making a noise." said Tobias and continued: "B'stard is downstairs, in the dining room, somewhere. Our little Indian friend is talking to him about his planned conquest!"

"**What!**" the other four exclaimed loudly, still holding the covers on their mouths, this time it was Tobias who shushed them;

"The trouble is" he said, "B'stard has used up at least one of the remaining two wishes"

A stunned silence followed as they tried to collect their thoughts. Tobias continued:

"I have worse news. Because he was unable to incant the correct incantation for world domination, he has found a far worse one, for us anyway."

"What's he wished for Toby?" asked O'nad.

"I remember when I was copying the original journal that there were all manner of useless incantations, interspersed with these were several really powerful ones – but you have to look hard, for they, and the journal, are written in a manner so as to conceal them, so as not to be found easily by the 'wrong person'" he paused; "I can't remember the actual incantation, but I know for a fact that he has wished for the ability to raise up an army of the dead!"

"A what?" Julia interjected.

"It is true!" followed O'nad; "I remember the actual incantation, specifically because of the strange words used to summon the army – "Byddin am y marw" – it's Welsh apparently, and combined with the short incant 'Isn't it not, look you, there's lovely', it summons the army." he went on.

"And what's more" continued Tobias "is that, as the incant indicates, the army will be made up entirely of Welsh people and, obviously, that depends on the number of dead Welsh people in the immediate vicinity"

"Obviously!" interrupted David, sarcastically. "But we're in Hartlepool, there can't be that many Welsh bodies in the cemeteries here?" he questioned.

"Quite true." answered Tobias "But the incantation fails to state how far back in time to go, so we could be talking as far back as two or three thousand years – there may well be an awful lot of people of Welsh descent in and around these parts, but what would be our worst nightmare, almost totally incomprehensible in its magnitude, is if B'stard decides to summon his army in Wales – imagine all the Welsh folk buried in Wales over the last few thousand years and you're talking of an army of millions!" he scarily concluded.

## Chapter 19
*"Relocation, Relocation"*

Anul's keenness to get started with issuing his commands, as well as doing 'other things', to an army of the dead was apparent but B'stard ordered caution, though for Anul a cold shower might have been more appropriate. B'stard knew full well that he had to get his timing just right before setting in place the sequence of events which would lead to the eventual need to summon the army. This was equally obvious to Anul, though he was blinded by his own perverted desires.

Despite this clear understanding both Anul and B'stard were also keen to determine the means of summoning, and then sending back, their army of the dead. Neither party knew that the army would be made up entirely of Welsh people, though B'stard had a vague idea that the phrase used to bring forth the army was possibly Gaelic in origin. They decided to hold a test summoning.

As they set off for a secure location – they had decided on one of the nearby disused factories (which in Hartlepool were easily found), B'stard was annoyed to find yet another horse and cart, possibly the same one, blocking his exit from his parking space in the car park opposite the hotel. Once again he removed the offending vehicle and set off, with Anul occupying the passenger seat. Safely secured in the boot of his Ford Fiesta were the journal and Heinny's testicle case. Soon they came upon an ex steel mill, the warehouse of which was as big as an aeroplane hangar and easily accessed through the heavily corroded wrought iron gates which bore the name 'British Steel'; checking the doors to the warehouse itself B'stard was once more agitated that they seemed to be heavily secured with sturdy brass padlocks and even stronger looking steel cable. An hour and thirty minutes later, after much sawing – using a nail file that he had secreted within one of is trench coat pockets, as well as his trusty, but severely worn, sword – they finally gained entry to the cavernous building.

Once inside B'stard immediately unpacked the journal and scrotal sac; turning to the page he had bookmarked and picking up the slowly decaying scrotum he began to recite the incantation to raise his army of the dead:

*"**Army of the Dead,***
*Get out of your bed,*
*Do as I say,*
*And follow what is said"*

He followed this with the words guaranteed to bring forth the zombie flesh-eating army:

*"Byddin am y marw -*
*Isn't it not, look you, there's lovely"*

"That should do it." he said. Anul was not convinced as, in the first instance, nothing was immediately apparent and secondly

# A Crofter's Tale (The REAL Story of The Hartlepool Monkey)

B'stard didn't seem to be convinced either. Seconds later both would have no doubts over the success of the incantation.

Initially a feint rumbling sound, like a car driving over a wooden bridge, pervaded the silence of the huge warehouse. Moments later a deep baritone voice could be heard booming out the words to 'Men of Harlech' and what sounded like hundreds of pairs of boot shod feet could also be heard clattering into the disused building. B'stard and Anul turned to where the sounds were coming from and stared in open mouthed astonishment as not one, not two, but four walking dead entered through the far end wall – not because they had the ability to walk through solid objects, but because there was a gaping hole within it – B'stard looked at Anul; Anul looked at B'stard, disappointment clearly etched on both of their faces; disappointment because of the disastrously low turnout of dead, for B'stard, and double disappointment at the fact that none of them were particularly attractive and all four of them were far too animated, for Anul. Despite his disappointment however, Anul was still enormously excited by the appearance of these dead folk; an excitement which meant he had to double himself up even more than usual. Years of death did not seem to have decayed the zombies before him, their clothing was normal, if a little dirty, and their skin bore the typical grey pallor associated with just a few hours of being dead. Anul was particularly impressed with the larger of the two males in the group.

The beautifully voiced leader of the gang of four spoke first, his deep voice amplified and resonating throughout the building,

"Pleased to meet you sir, Dai Evans at your service isn't it, Dai being a particularly apt name, given that I've been dead these past eighty seven years look you." he chuckled, "died in a minin' accident see, but was buried in Hartlepool because of an administrative error, isn't it!"

A Crofter's Tale (The REAL Story of The Hartlepool Monkey)

B'stard tersely nodded a greeting, still reeling from the massive disappointment at the appearance of his 'army', one of the other 'zombies' spoke up next;

*"Hello"* she said, *"I'm Gladys Evans see, Dai's wife, and these two are our little ones, Gwyneth and Evan, look you, isn't it. We couldn't leave 'im buried up 'ere on his own, see, so we all moved up here isn't it. Lived 'ere 'til we died of starvation during the depression isn't it."*

B'stard couldn't hide his annoyance any longer and screamed at the army of four, "I hope to Christ there are more of you than this! Please tell me the rest of the army is waiting outside or something!" he enquired without asking.

*"Steady there now, isn't it! Not in front of the children if you please Sir!"* responded Dai, *"I'm afraid we're all you've got see. You've summoned an army of the dead from the Valleys haven't you, look you? By a cruel twist of fate, for you, we're the only Welsh people buried in Hartlepool see? We Welsh folk are a proud nation and wouldn't, ordinarily, be seen dead in a place like Hartlepool; had it not been for the administrative error you wouldn't have even had us. If you'd wanted a bigger army you should've gone to Wales boyyo, isn't it; loads of dead Welsh people in Wales I would imagine, isn't there, I mean it!"* he said, sarcastically, with that B'stard let out a huge scream of rage, which echoed around the building, startling a nest of pigeons who flew off through the hole in the wall;

"Why in god's name did they have to be bloody Welsh? Couldn't I just have a simple, common-or-garden Army of the Dead?"

"Is there such a thing, Master?" questioned Anul; B'stard, realising the inanity of his question, ignored him and continued to rant,

"What the hell am I supposed to do with a family of dead Welshies?" he bellowed.

# A Crofter's Tale (The REAL Story of The Hartlepool Monkey)

"Send them back Sir" said Anul, "Send them back, and when we need the army, we'll go to Wales to summon another one, one much bigger." he paused, "and one with a lot more people of a male persuasion in it." he added; colossal pervert as he was, not even Anul could contemplate Grande Necromancy on Dai's wife for, despite the obvious fact of her being dead, she was just too female, and Anul never touched children, preferring to leave that to what he classed as, the 'really sick bastards'.

*"That would, under normal circumstances, be a relatively good idea, Sir"* uttered Dai, *"But, look you, these are not normal circumstances, isn't it; once we've been summoned we can't be sent back see, so I'm afraid you're stuck with us, isn't it. We could always take you to the valleys later on, to summon more Welsh stiffs for you though, look you."* Anul was forced to bend forward a little further at the mention of the word 'stiff', and now became increasingly likely to topple over through being top-heavy;

"Is that possible?" queried B'stard

"Of course, Sir, I wouldn't say it if it wasn't. You can summon as many times as you want see, but you can never send any of them, us, back, but don't worry Sir, we don't take much looking after see, us not having the stomach for food anymore, isn't it!" he laughed. B'stard at last saw the funny side of things and let out an enormously hideous and dastardly cackle, which was made even more hideous and dastardly by the echo of the warehouse, he was closely followed by Anul, whose lungs, being compressed by the weight of his hunch, which was accentuated due to his excited crouched stance, could only emit a sort of hissing sound through his closed teeth, making him sound very much like Mutley the dog; and so it was, Anul, B'stard and The Evans' made their way back to The Dosser's Arms Hotell. (L+L=2L).

At the hotel with two 'l's' O'nad, Heinny and Tobias were still rummaging through B'stard's belongings, searching for Heinny's ball sack. Even though one of the wishes had been used up, and it was therefore reasonable to assume that B'stard had found a suitable incantation to use up the third and final one, there was still a chance that the baboon could be reunited with his male appendages, if only for cosmetic purposes. Search as they might, they were destined to fail in this particular quest.

David and Julia Snaith had gone back downstairs to wait in the dining room of the hotel for B'stard and his Sikh friend to come back. Obviously none of the three who remained up stairs could have been given this task as they were all known to B'stard, either through sight or legend; O'nad had agreed with Tobias that B'stard had most likely uttered the cloak of invisibility incantation, and was, quite probably, still downstairs, invisible. Had B'stard recognised those waiting for him, within the dining room of the hotel, the outcome of this tale could have been enormously different, possibly even slightly better.

The Snaiths sat in the less than comfortable, and even worse than less than clean, sofa in the stinking dining room; to all intents and purposes they looked just like any ordinary, working class, and therefore particularly impoverished, young couple on holiday; David hid behind a copy of The Hartlepool Mail, whose front page screamed out the major news of the day – **'New Jobs Boost for Hartlepool'**, with the sub header "Betting shop extension creates two new cleaning posts in Owton Manor." David was reading the deaths column; Julia had a copy of 'Benefit News' from the local Job Centre, which proudly announced the same two cleaning jobs as a 'major boost' to the local economy as well as featuring an article on the Incapacity Benefit Department's latest underwater breathing assessment for COPD sufferers.

The couple did not speak at first for fear of inadvertently giving the game away or giving B'stard reason to believe that something was afoot. Instead, both David and Julia simply monitored the seat on which they knew B'stard to be patiently waiting (noticeable purely by the indentations of their enemy's buttock cheeks). The silence was, however, broken by David;

"Nice weather we're having dear!"

"Yes, yes it is darling. What shall we do today?" Julia dutifully responded. This inane, and typically British chatting, went on for a few minutes more. B'stard, continuing to remain invisible to the seemingly innocent Snaiths, sat back and eaves dropped their mundane conversation. It was enough for B'stard to assume that the persons here present were of no threat and gave him no reason to believe there was something he should be wary about. With this B'stard quickly dismissed the couple's presence and ceased his curious eaves dropping activities. To B'stard, it was as if the Snaiths did not exist at all.

Just then the hunchbacked Sikh appeared in the room. He hobbled across the shiny carpet. The carpet was shiny, not because of the luxurious make-up of the textiles used in its construction, but rather because of the decades of filth that it had absorbed, with any form of cleaning intervention, causing a quarter of an inch film of petrified gunge to coat the once perfect fibres. It was enough for anyone attempting to traverse the length of the carpeted room to keep their balance and not slip upon the greasy surface. Perhaps this explained why the 'cleaners' were often seen wearing ice-skates whilst going about their 'cleaning' duties. This way the 'domestic maintenance personnel' could fair whizz across the rink (carpet) in the pursuit of their daily duties. Anul had successfully reached the table, at which B'stard was patiently waiting, without coming a cropper on the way. He sat down and furtively looked around. Anul observed the presence of the Snaiths and further observed that they were engaged in meaningless conversation. He, like B'stard, dismissed their presence and went about addressing his master in a whispered tone.

"My Lord, the incantation and your prophecy are true! With the army of the dead and your cloak of invisibility at our disposal we must now quicken our intentions to make good your destiny and take over the world."

B'stard's response was equally hushed

"You are right my servant. But in order to fulfil this we must first travel to a most hideous place, a place where a 'true' and formidable Army can be resurrected. The place in question is so vile and abhorrent that only the strongest and fool-hardy would dare to travel; this place is renowned for its inhospitable environment, especially to all those foreign to the land in question; a place where strange tongues and dialect are spoken that no outsider can fathom the meaning. Only in this place can we resurrect the Army we need for our heinous purposes".

Anul replied "You mean Wales don't you?"

"Yes, yes I do but more specifically I mean Mold." responded B'stard. "Only there can we summon a fury suitable for our purposes and not here in Hartlepool where the best we could muster was the pathetic Evans clan. Incidentally Anul, where are the Evans? What have you done with them?"

"Oh, I just told them to wait until they receive orders from me. Between me and you they'll be waiting for a long time...!" asserted Anul. Needless to say this is the last we will hear of the Evans' in our tale but readers beware, if you do come across a Welsh family in the Hartlepool area be careful, very careful. They are, after all Welsh!

The conversation between B'stard and Anul continued around the theme of their imminent sojourn to Wales. All the time the pair whispered their plans so as to keep it secure from unwanted ears.

Now, to normal people, their whispered tones would have been inaudible, even to the Snaiths who were seated approximately 20 feet from the devious pair. However, the Snaiths cannot be labelled with the term 'normal', specifically Julia. It is fair to say that women, in general, have far better hearing than men and that most women can hear a pin drop from up to 500 miles away

# A Crofter's Tale (The REAL Story of The Hartlepool Monkey)

(especially if that 'pin-drop' is 'gossip related'). Julia is no exception to this feminine trait. Not only does Julia possess one buttock which is 50% larger than its counterpart and that this ratio is replicated in her breasts but she also possesses ears which are of phenomenal proportions. Each pinna extends 2 inches out from her temples with a 6 inch span from the top of each ear to the lobe. Julia possesses jugs in abundance. These traits served to prove useful as she was readily able to hear every softly spoken word uttered by the mysterious Sikh and his 'hidden' friend.

Julia maintained the meaningless banter with her husband, all the time absorbing the detail of the conversation being held outside of her husband's own hearing threshold. Julia had heard enough and got to her feet.

"Come on love, lets go for a walk." she said to David.
David joined his jug-eared wife and they both left the dining room. Anul and B'stard remained to carry on with the detail.

Once outside the dining room both Julia and David made for the reception area where Tobias, O'nad and Heinny were covertly hiding.

"What news Julia?" asked Heinny.

"Oh, there's plenty of news but it's too dangerous to talk here." responded Julia. "Quick, let's get out of here so we can discuss it all." she said, and with that our heroes left the hotel and boarded O'nad's cart to await the latest information from their friend.

Julia relayed all that she had overheard from B'stard and his evil Sikh henchman. She explained that B'stard was hiding, courtesy of a 'cloak of invisibility', and that this ability was surely one of the two wishes he had the ability to avail himself of; she also explained the plans to summon the Army of the Dead in a place called Mold in North Wales. O'nad and Tobias looked at each other and concurred that they had indeed guessed correctly about cloak of invisibility; at least our friends now knew what they were dealing with. The only question which now remained was how to tackle and stop B'stard before he could wreak havoc. It was far too late to stop B'stard from simply reeking for he had spent too long in the grubby Dosser's Arms, but they still had a moral obligation to stop him from wreaking.

## Chapter 20
*"McNad Returns Again"*

"Right!" bellowed Heinny. "We know where he is, even if we can't see him, and we know where he's about to go; I say we storm back in that place and stomp on his fucking invisible head to put a stop to this right here, right now".

The rest of the group agreed with Heinny's carefully thought out strategy and raced back into the Dosser's Arms Hotell screaming and shouting obscenities as they proceeded. David lagged behind shouting

"I'll cover the rear." David is a colossal wimp who knows only how to belittle and bully his wife and other women, but dare not confront another male. However, when they got to the dining room there wasn't a single, solitary soul to be found, not even Anul (who lacked the ability to shroud himself with a cloak of invisibility).

"Damn, they've gone!" exclaimed Heinny in a disappointed tone.

"Good job really, 'cause I was just about to kick some serious ass" pronounced David.

"Of course you were darling." said his wife condescendingly.

"What are we going to do now?" asked Heinny.

"Well, to me there's only one thing we can do my simian friend. We're going to have to squeeze your bollock once more." replied O'nad. The others winced at the idea and Heinny suddenly felt quite queasy.

"But Heinny hasn't got any bollocks." said Julia. "I should know I've had a bloody good rummage down there." she went on to add. True to form David said nothing.

"You are mistaken Julia. Remember we do have one of Heinny's love eggs in our possession. The magical orienteering orb." explained O'nad.

"Oh yes, the magical orb" said Julia. "Hasn't done much yet has it?" she added.

"You are quite mistaken Julia." said O'nad. "The teste has already helped us once by telling us that B'stard was staying here at the Dosser's Arms Hotell. So you see it has already proved to be a useful tool in our quest." added O'nad.

"What do you mean 'told us'?" asked Julia.

"Heinny's bollock has an alter ego. This 'other' being is called McNad." "He's right Julia." added Heinny. "I've got a wee Scotsman living in one of my nuts. He goes by the name of McNad and he's divulged everything that O'nad has told you to date. I've yet to meet him personally but I'm told he's as friendly as he is helpful." with this Heinny looked to O'nad for affirmation. However, O'nad knowing McNad as he did simply shrugged his shoulders said "The little scotch egg's alright when you get to know him, trust me!"

"So how do we get in touch with this McNad character again?" asked Tobias.

"Like I said Toby we simply squeeze Heinny's gonad and he will appear."

This was all too much for Heinny, what with all this talk of squeezing his gonads, who proceeded to faint and drop to the floor with a simian thud. Julia dutifully (as Julia always did) attended to

# A Crofter's Tale (The REAL Story of The Hartlepool Monkey)

Heinny, stroking his face and his groin, but it would be sometime before he would regain consciousness.

"Permit me to demonstrate." offered O'nad as he removed Heinny's testicle from his jacket pocket. Slipping out of his Wellington boots, he reached into his bag and brought out the pair of shiny, diamante encrusted shoes, which he proceeded to slip onto his feet; the others stared in wonder as O'nad, once more, clicked his shiny heels together three times. With that O'nad placed the orb in his outstretched palm so as to show everyone that it was indeed someone else's testicle he was holding. Everyone looked on in anticipation as the once outstretched palm of O'nad's hand started to close into a tightly clenched fist. Everyone, with the exception of Julia, began to sweat profusely whilst simultaneously crossing their legs as they witnessed this curious act.

Suddenly, and as if from nowhere, came a gravelly and grumpy voice

*"Whet the farks go-arn on the noo ya bassas?"* All could hear but none could see. That was until O'nad began to loosen his grip on the orb and reveal the transformed occupant within. With arm outstretched everyone (except the unconscious Heinny) could now see the strange character standing centrally in O'nad's hand.

*"Twice in as many days yev summoned me; mark ye well there'll be nay mer than thrice times! Yee'd betta have a good reason tae wake me ya banch a freeks or ya'll have ya heed in ya harnds so ya wull."* snarled the bad tempered testicle.

"Sorry Mr McNad but it appears that B'stard has given us the slip once again." exclaimed O'nad.

*"Fa farks sake, ya're banch o useless bassas aren't ya!"* shouted McNad. The testicular form went on to say *"The woman's told yae where he's gone and that place is Mold. All ya have tae dee is tae follow hem. Once there only then well he reveal his true entenshuns for he needs to see the might of his Armay o deed peepal. But mark ye well, yae need to use stealth and make sure he does nae see you for this may prove your undoing. Now fek off and*

*let mae be!"* With this McNad disappeared in a puff of epidydimus.

The group pondered what McNad had advised them and agreed that they should continue to pursue B'stard to the end of the earth (Wales) to monitor his next steps. O'nad was aware of the fact that on the two occasions he had had need for McNad's services, the little Elgin marble had told them precisely what they already knew; he made a mental note not to call him again unless there was a real requirement to do so. He slipped off the shiny red shoes surreptitiously and returned them to his bag. With this Heinny regained consciousness and asked what had happened. Julia explained that his gonad had given them all the information they would need and that all that remained was for them to make haste in their journey to Wales. It appeared to Heinny that he would never see his testicle at this rate for every time it appeared he was either out of the room or in a state of unconsciousness.

"Well, I suppose we'd best make tracks." said O'nad.

"Yes, Wales or Bust!" replied Tobias.

# Chapter 21
## *"The A Team Set Off"*

The famous five left the Dosser's Arms Hotell for what they hoped would be the last time. Their experiences at this godforsaken place had been nothing short of nightmarish. The hotel and indeed Hartlepool could easily be mistaken for Helll. ('L' cubed).

Once outside O'nad quickly clapped his hands three times in quick succession as he went about summoning his trusty cart.

This was more than Heinny, Julia and Tobias could take and they all blurted out in unison

"Not the sodding cart again, please!"

The group needed to make their way to Mold, which was some 200 miles from their present position. They had only just gotten over the mammoth and entirely unnecessarily long journey that took them from London to Hartlepool and that had taken nearly three weeks! They couldn't go through that again. David said nothing but simply kicked his heels whilst his companions argued about the archaic mode of transport. Not wishing to become embroiled in the transportation debate David took himself off explaining that he *needed to 'spend a penny'*, It was an action that David would soon regret.

In David's absence the group complained that his 'aversion' to all things automotive was serving simply to cause hindrance to the progress of their quest. They considered leaving him behind as he was, after all, useless and had brought nothing to the group to date. O'nad however, reminded the rest of the group that this was not an option as the prophecy foretold that the 'Snaiths' would bring balance to the sacred testicle (emphasising the pleural, as he coughed violently, producing a huge 'pavement oyster' which would indicate that he was suffering with an infection of the pleural membrane, thus producing a surplus of 'lung butter'; though meaning plural and not singular). Therefore David needed to be very much a part of the travelling band. Julia tutted her disappointment, as did the rest of the group until they finally conceded that leaving the useless get behind was ***not*** an option.

"There must be another option surely?" asked Heinny, not one for giving up so easily.

"I told you what we should have done even before we left London." Said Julia.

"What was that?" responded her beloved simian.

"Knock him out."

"Brilliant!" said Heinny and the rest of the group cheered in unanimous agreement.

"How are we to do it and, more to the point, who will do it?" pronounced Tobias.

"Oh, that's easy," reacted Julia. "I'll do it!" she added.

"OK, so we have a volunteer but again I must ask the question how do we do it?" said Tobias. Julia hadn't given this aspect much thought. All she knew was she wanted to render her husband unconscious.

"We need something big and heavy, maybe with a big spike." Said Heinny and all at once our heroes (minus David of course who was still micturating) found themselves scouring the car-park for any debris that would prove useful for their intended act of ABH (Actual Bodily Harm). Incidentally, at this point no one stopped to consider the moral aspect of the act they were about to perpetrate. Instead they all tacitly decided that he had it coming to him anyway and this was more than enough justification for the act in question. All at once Julia spotted the ideal implement. It was big, it was heavy, and it even came with a big spike. It was a three foot length of two by four with a six inch nail protruding from the top. It was probably constructed by one of the locals as a makeshift 'self-defence' tool. Either that or it was a child's play thing, after all this type of toy was 'all the craze' in Hartlepool for the Christmas that had just passed. Julia picked up the timber and iron constructed article and passed it from hand to hand as if to calibrate it's centre of gravity and to establish how best to wield the offending object. All the time Julia was doing this she smiled to herself and her companions and proclaimed;

"This is just the ticket!"

David had finished his urinary evacuation and returned to the group. It was obvious to the group what he'd been up to as a stain had appeared on his light coloured pants. The stain in question was circular in shape and around four inches in diameter.

The epicentre of the stain appeared to be emanating from his groin and more specifically from an area that would have been housing his glans. The stain was piss, for it was a piss stain. David, clearly embarrassed by this made excuses and said that a Dog had been sniffing at his crotch leaving a wet residue in the aforementioned area. The actual words David used were that *"It wasn't piss, but a puppy's nose."*

Not remotely interested in what David had to say Heinny piped up "We've all decided to make our journey (pointing to each member of the group, one by one) by car as we have no time to lose if we are to get to B'stard in time." David turned ashen and stuttered the words

"I don't fucking think s……" Before David could finish his sentence Julia brought the 'child's toy' down upon his head with all her might (if truth be known the force she used was excessive, even to Heinny and the other onlookers).

"I seem to remember this happening to Mr T (BA Baracus) every week on the A Team if the others wanted to get him on a plane." said Julia as she stood over her fallen husband.

"You are right Julia, but didn't they employ drugs as the preferred method rather than an act of wanton barbarism?" responded O'nad.

"Yes they did but we don't have any drugs and anyway this is much more fun." she retorted.

The group became conscious of time whilst David remained unconscious. He lay, seemingly dead, whilst the others decided their next move. Only Tobias had the decency to check for vital signs. He was breathing, barely! A close inspection of David showed that Julia's aim was near prefect, near being the operative word for had she been any nearer her husband would surely be dead, for the six inch nail had embedded itself (almost entirely) into his skull. This meant that David was attached to the three foot piece of two by four by its protruding metal fastener. Tobias dared not attempt to remove the offending object in case he compromised David's existence and instead left him to his erratic breathing.

The group decided to secure a car by honest means. After all they were all law abiding citizens (except for Julia who now had 'form') and O'nad had the financial means to purchase even the most luxurious of automotive transportation. And so it was decided that they would go to the nearest car dealership and purchase a new car for cash to go! (This is easier said than done at most, if not all car dealerships as they would much prefer you take the finance option but for the purposes of this tale we must assume that it is possible in Hartlepool). Fortunately a car dealership was conveniently sited adjacent to the car-park in which they were assembled. Armed with fists full of cash and a near dead companion the odd-looking troop trooped off towards the dealership.

Now, our friends were going to purchase a top of the range estate car but were advised, by the salesman, that a people carrier might be more suitable. Not that the estate option could not easily transport all five of our heroes but because of the 'additional luggage' that also needed to be transported. The 'additional luggage' being the large piece of tree that David was sporting as the latest in fashionable headwear.

The deal was done and the people carrier was purchased. David was crammed into the back (quite literally) his head slightly protruding causing the door not to be able to be closed with any ease. Julia stepped in to assist and proceeded to slam the car door against her husband's haemorrhaging cranium until finally they were able to 'safely' secure David into the vehicle.

With a full tank of petrol and a quiet road ahead of them they set off, Satellite Navigation assisted to Mold, North Wales.

## Chapter 22
*"The Journey to Mold"*

After 170.7 miles, and only 3hrs and 1 minute travelling time, our heroes arrived at their destination.

**The End**

(Well, for the journey at least).

## Chapter 23
*"Mouldy Old Mold"*

Our heroes pulled up, in their new people carrier, at a lay-by in the apparently deserted centre of Mold. The journey had taken its toll on the passengers who now felt that they needed to alight and stretch their legs. Heinny's testicle had become numb during the journey, not because he'd been sitting on it but because O'nad had! Julia was the first to get out of the car followed by Heinny, Onad and then Tobias. David was still slumped across the back seat, as he had been throughout the entire trip. Within moments of arriving the 'conscious' members of the team had barely had chance to take their first deep breath of Welsh air when David began to rouse.

"Quick!" ushered Julia. "He's waking up, we need to get him out of the car or he'll have a fit (quite literally given his life threatening aversion to all things automotive), Heinny help me." she added.

Heinny and Julia, before David could regain full consciousness, dragged the forlorn looking character from the blood stained back seats. O'nad instantly knew what he had to do if the group wanted to keep their dark secret from David. He clapped his hands together in quick succession and all at once there stood the infamous cart (which was despised by all except for O'nad and, of course, David). Heinny and Julia had barely dragged David but four or five yards from the vehicle when he uttered his first, groggily spoken words.

"Christ on a bicycle, my fucking head, It's absolutely banging! Where am I, er, where are we?"

"We're in Mold, in North Wales." answered his wife.

"Hang on a minute, how did we get here then? The last thing I remember was taking a piss in Hartlepool."

"That's right dear but when you finished you tripped, had a nasty fall, and knocked yourself out. You've been completely out of it for the entire journey."

"But how did we get here so quickly." David once again asked, this time in a rather suspicious way.

"By cart of course!" said O'nad as he pointed to his beloved chariot.

"It took us three weeks to travel from London to Hartlepool when we first set out on this farce. Wales must be just as long a journey as that one. Are you telling me I've been unconscious for 3 weeks?"

The others looked at each other in a rather guilty and coy way then turned to David. Heinny said "Yes, you have."

"Fucking hell" replied David. "That would explain this banging headache then!"

The group helped David to his feet and, as if by natural reflex, David lifted his hand up to his head (obviously in an attempt to massage the pain away or to carry out an inspection of some sort). Julia quickly said.

"I wouldn't touch that if I were you dear. You've got a nasty 'bump' there and you don't want to go and aggravate it do you?"

"But my head, it feels so heavy. It feels like I'm carrying a ton weight on it. Can I at least have a look in a mirror or something?" he winced.

"Oh, David you're such a drama queen. Just leave it alone and it will get better in its own. Trust me it's only a scratch!" David sighed but did as his wife instructed, after all he didn't want the others to think he was a bit of a 'nancy-boy'.

With a now fully conscious David the group huddled together in the lay-by to discuss their next moves. O'nad was the first to suggest what they needed to do. He did this by reminding the group what McNad had told them.

"McNad said we should travel to Mold, and now we're here! He told us to covertly track our enemy and his deformed cohort so as to maintain the element of surprise but primarily in order to find out what their plans are for coming to this godforsaken place is." The group looked at O'nad and nodded. They did this as a universally recognised indication of understanding. David tried to nod but lost his balance (reasons being quite apparent) and once again fell over and banged his head. Heinny, being the shrewd simian that he was, seized the opportunity that now stood before him. He lifted David to his feet once more and announced to him

"Bloody hell David that was a nasty fall! You seem to have inadvertently fallen on a three foot piece of two by four timber with a six inch nail protruding from it and now it's almost entirely embedded in your skull. You know, you must be more careful!" Julia concurred with Heinny (as did the rest of the group) but was unable to conceal her laughter. David's only response was "That's all I fucking need, just my luck!"

"What now then O'nad?" asked Tobias.

"Well, we know that B'stard is invisible to us as he has the cloak that makes him so. He will probably remain in this state for as long as possible. However, if we are to locate him in this place we must look for his partner, the Sikh."

"Shouldn't be too much trouble." replied Tobias. "There can't be that many Sikhs in Mold, surely. Well not of the hunchback variety anyhow."

"You are right Tobias." said O'nad.

O'nad had barely finished his sentence when the quiet streets of Mold town centre suddenly transformed. The group could hear music! Yet this music didn't sound as if it belonged in Wales, its tune was more 'eastern' (perhaps Bradford, thought Julia). They looked around to see where the melodious tunes were coming from. Then all at once the source was revealed. Coming down the street and in their general direction was a marching Sikh hoard!

"Bollocks, I forgot about this." said O'nad. "It's the 23$^{rd}$ of May isn't it?" he added. David verified this by nodding.

"Its only Guru Amar Das's birthday isn't it?"

"Who?" exclaimed Heinny.

"Guru Amar Das. He was the third of the Sikh Gurus born 1479 and died 1574. The celebration of a Guru's birthday is a huge event to all Sikhs"

"Oh, this just gets fucking better this does!" shouted David. "We've come all this way looking for the invisible man and his sideshow freak, the Sikh. We can't see B'stard, obviously, and now we've got Sikhs coming out of our frigging ears!" he frustratingly retorted.

"O'nad, how come you know so much about Sikhs?" asked Heinny. "When you've lived as long as I have you learn a lot of useful facts, and anyhow the poster behind you (pointing to an extremely large billboard) gives you all the confirmation you need." They all looked around at the aforementioned billboard and universally exclaimed; "Oh yeh, so it does!"

"I know it's a bit coincidental what with us being here looking for a Sikh in a town not particularly famed for its abundance of persons of this faith, but remember we're looking for just one, a hunchback one at that. This will make him stand out like a sore thumb. Therefore it's not a thankless task after all." added O'nad.

"Yes, you're right O'nad." said Tobias. "Let's go and begin our search." With that the group approached the celebrating throng to start their search.

"What they bloody hell……." gasped Heinny. The others all looked at Heinny to see what he was referring to. Heinny simply pointed at the passing throng whilst simultaneously shaking his head in disbelief. The others all looked in the direction that their friend was pointing. Mouths wide open in total surprise David announced;

"They're all hunchbacks! They're all frigging hunchbacks!" David started to cry and laugh at the same time, the events unfolding were too much for his frail mental state to comprehend or take in. Heinny once again looked at the poster displayed on the billboard. Sure enough there, and for the entire world to see (well Mold at least) was the strap line;

***"The Mold Hunchback Sikh Society Proudly Presents"***
[Apparently, Mold has the largest population of spinally deformed Asians in the entire world – though it is thought that Prestatyn runs a close second].

"Calm down David!" said his wife. "We're looking for one that is seemingly talking to himself. This should be easy to spot, and if we find him we've also found B'stard."

"Genius!" pronounced Heinny (always willing to give Julia praise and 'other' things).

"Let's get among them and look for the one who is having a singular conversation!" announced O'nad. However, things would appear to go from bad to worse at this point for it would appear that every hunchbacked Sikh, the group came across, was talking to himself. The group, being totally demoralised and dejected, left the sprawling throng of 'gibbering' Asians and headed back towards the lay-by. Heinny once again looked at the postered billboard. The answer was, once again, staring him (and his friends) in the face. The strap line had an additional piece of information beneath it. The information was captured in brackets and read

***("The Schizophrenic Arm")***

Surely our heroes luck, and indeed patience, was fast running out.

However, just as quickly as their luck had diminished it returned; for out of the Asian celebratory throng came a lone Sikh. The Sikh was hunchbacked (as were they all) and he was muttering to himself (again, as they all were) but this Sikh drew the attentions of our heroes for he was muttering the word *"B'stard"* every so often; there was no mention on the billboard poster referencing that the Sikh hunchbacked, schizophrenic, party were affiliated to the 'Tourettes society'. This surely meant that their search for the elusive Sikh was over. This was further confirmed when our heroes heard the reply

*"Quickly Anul we must make haste for the graveyard. Time is precious and my Army awaits me."* It was B'stard.

O'nad et al retreated, so as not to be seen by the heinous pair. Anul and B'stard headed off down the street and past a road-sign displaying ***"Mold Cemetery 250yrds"***. When our heroes were satisfied that they were of sufficient distance from the pair (so as not to cause any suspicion of being tailed) they set off in pursuit. David, as usual, lagged behind, not because he was a consummate coward but because of the extra 'baggage' he was now carrying.

## Chapter 24
*"The Graveyard"*

B'stard and Anul entered the gates of Mold Cemetery. B'stard was, by now, growing with excitement. He had also quoted the words *"just like that"* which made him visible once more. Anul, too, was equally excited but his was 'groaning' rather than growing. B'stard's excitement forced him to become fidgety as he rummaged through his trouser pockets looking for the incantation that would bring forth his 'New Welsh Army'. Anul was also fidgety and he too rummaged the contents of his pocket. Anul, however, had no incantation to locate and so we can only assume that he was masturbating once more (being the colossal pervert that he is).

"At last!" said B'stard. "I can now summon the might of my Army." And with that he unfolded the piece of paper which held the phrase he would need to incant in order to bring forth his abominations. All the time O'nad and crew observed from afar (actually they observed from just inside the cemetery gates which was far enough). B'stard held up the piece of paper so that its contents could be illuminated by the moonlight. B'stard would have to wait some considerable time for this to happen as it had just turned noon. A break in the clouds let in an intense ray of sunlight which served to light up the paper (in a way that far in excess betters that which the moon could have done). Without a moment to lose B'stard quoted the hastily scrawled words ***"Isn't it now look you, there's lovely",*** whilst simultaneously squeezing the scrotal sac.

Seconds later the earth began to tremble. It shook as if it were about to rend itself open before their very eyes. B'stard and Anul looked around and could observe a passing JCB Bulldozer on its way to the Council Works Yard which lay opposite the cemetery. The roads surrounding the cemetery were in a poor state of disrepair and this caused the bulldozer to 'kangaroo' all the way down the uneven surface of the road on which it was travelling. This explained the noise and B'stard simply tutted in disapproval.

Anul thought B'stard should repeat his incantation and proffered that "The dead might not have heard you over the noise of the bulldozer." B'stard tutted once more and replied "Imbecile!" None the less, B'stard spoke the words once more.

This time things were slightly different. Rather than hearing the ground rumbling he heard the sound of what seemed like high pressured air escaping from a small aperture. Anul had just broken wind and this brought forth a stench that one could have easily mistaken for a rotten corpse. Just as B'stard was about to berate his second in command (a post he would, no doubt, live to regret ever giving him) a mass of voices could be heard mumbling *"There's lovely, isn't it now look you"* and *"Whose coat is this jacket"* (both phrases being delivered in a stereotypical Welsh twang).

B'stard turned to face the source of the mumblings and there, before him and his Asian friend, stood hundreds of gormless and catatonic looking Welsh folk.

"You must be my Army of the Dead?" proclaimed B'stard.

"You are dead aren't you?" he added.

*"Oh yes boyyo we're dead all right, isn't it"* came a drone from one of figures lurking at the front of the assembled mass.

"Good, just checking. It's so difficult to gauge with the Welsh." responded B'stard "I suppose the foul stench that you bring with you from your graves is enough to confirm my question?" added B'stard.

"Sorry my Lord, that's me again." said Anul as he let rip another sour rectal flatulent evacuation.

"Christ Anul what the fuck have you been eating?" said B'stard.

"I had an English last night and it's playing havoc with my lower intestine. I don't think 'bland' food agrees with me." replied Anul apologetically.

"It doesn't agree with me either you dirty swine. Just give a little advance notice next time will you?"

"Right you are sire!" agreed the Sikh.

Turning his attentions back to his dead troops (their 'zombified' status having now been confirmed despite them being Welsh) B'stard announced "Now listen to me for I am your Lord and Master. You will do as I say and act as I will you to. We have much work to do and that work will take us to the seat of British power – The Houses of Parliament. Once there you will take further orders. For now all you need to know is that my word is law!"

"Aren't you forgetting something?" asked Anul. B'stard instantly knew what Anul was referring to and said

"I'm getting to that bit." He turned once more to his stupefied minions and added "This is Anul. Anul Abu-Sar. He is my Second in Command and as such you will also take orders from him. Do as both Anul and I say. Do I make myself clear?" he bellowed. The assembled mass of zombies replied in unison and drawled the word *"Yakee-dar"*. This was enough for B'stard who was familiar with the works of Max Boyce and knew this 'word' as something which denotes a positive response.

Meanwhile, O'nad and company continued to conceal their presence. They watched on as the zombies complied with the commands of their new masters.

"Looks like were back on the road again." said David despairingly "Back to London were we fucking started!" he added angrily.

"Shushh, cloth head they'll hear us." urged Julia. Reluctantly, but nonetheless dutifully, David complied with Julia's request. He also wished he had a cloth head as it probably would be less painful than the one he was currently toting around.

"Let us start our journey." ordered B'stard as he addressed his newly formed brigade.

"Actually, before we set off I'd like to give that one" (pointing to a well proportioned zombie – probably an ex rugby player) "some personal orders." said Anul. "I'll be about five minutes, if that's alright?"

"If you absolutely must." responded B'stard. With that Anul disappeared with the groaning recently departed Welshman behind a tombstone. Anul was true to his word and five minutes later he returned, with the zombie (whose groans had curiously transformed in both tone and pitch as they were noticeably higher) to join the rest of the battalion.

"Finished have we?" asked B'stard.

"Yes thank you, but I'd like to give them all some personal orders between now and getting to London. You know, just to make sure they know what they are doing if you catch my drift?" he added.

B'stard thought Anul was being particularly professional and thorough in his approach to his post as second in command and this pleased him immensely. His pleasure was, however, short-lived as he then witnessed his henchman zipping up the fly of his trousers. B'stard now knew what Anul meant by some 'personal' orders. After B'stard had vomited in disgust he announced once more that their journey should begin immediately and they all set off marching (well shuffling, as zombies and hunchbacks do; in fact the only person capable of marching was B'stard) towards the cemetery gates.

"Sir?" asked Anul.

"What is it now?" came the reply.

"How are we going to get to London? It's some distance you know and travelling with a thousand welsh zombies is going to attract a little attention isn't it?"

"You are quite right Anul and it is for that reason we are travelling by British Rail. Only through this archaic mode of transport will we avoid any suspicions, such is the calibre of commuter that uses this method of transport".

"Gosh, you are clever." replied Anul. "What about the fares though?" "I've thought of that also and I've secured ample 'super-saver' tickets for us." (Just in case there are any readers pedantic enough to question how a group of zombies may legitimately travel on the railways without being rumbled as 'fare-dodgers').

Eventually and after every question had been asked and answered surrounding the Army's advance on the capital they set off and passed through the gates of the cemetery and onto the railway station. O'nad and party followed them in ninja like fashion.

"Anyone got any money for the train fares?" asked Julia.

"Yes, plenty" O'nad reminded her. David then piped up;

"Trains are a little like cars aren't they...?" The group knew what was coming next and instead of trying to put David's mind at peace Julia picked up a nearby plant-pot and sent it crashing, once more, across his head (being particularly careful not to hit the same spot as was now occupied by the two by four). David was out cold (again) and Heinny slung him, in a baboon like fashion across his shoulder and set forth, with the others, in the direction of Mold railway station.

## Chapter 25
*"London" (also spelt s-h-i-t-h-o-l-e)*

The journey from Mold to London is usually an uneventful one for British Rail; a single carriage is laid on to ferry those lucky enough to be leaving the Welsh town. Return tickets are very seldom sold at Mold Railway Station and, even more rarely is the single carriage filled. However, following a bizarre rush for tickets, the rail company had been forced to lay on an additional forty two coaches plus two buffet cars, in the hope that they could make the route profitable for the first time in thirty eight years. The reasons for the extra carriages was clearly due to the fact that B'stard and Anul had booked 1002 seats, though a further two hundred seats had also been booked by one hundred members of the Mold Hunchbacked Sikh Society (schizophrenic arm). The buffet cars had been duly stocked with sufficient 'food' to sustain their passengers along the way and, if sold, it would sustain British Rail for another ten minutes. (The term 'food' is used loosely as it's a pretty inadequate description for the cling filmed and sweating comestibles.) Sadly, for British Rail, they would fail to sell a single item from either of the two buffet cars, despite the journey being over five hours in duration, and despite the fact that, towards the end of the trek, they had reduced the selling price of each item to just £7.50 plus VAT plus service charge, in a desperate bid to rid themselves of the out of date, rancid, stock. By the end of the journey British Rail had become 'Railtrack'. Railtrack had bought the hazardous stock and would continue to sell it for the next four months.

A Crofter's Tale (The REAL Story of The Hartlepool Monkey)

The train departed Mold Railway Station at 13:08, just two hours later than scheduled due, in the main, to the fact that one of the Sikh society members could not, and apparently never did, locate his 'friend', and made good progress towards its destination. The clearly overstretched, and underpaid, ticket collector began his rounds at 13:09 starting with O'nad and our other heroes. Being the alert and conscientious employee he was he became frustrated that David, who was sprawled across two seats behind the rest of the gang, did not seem to respond to his barely audible demand for him to reveal his ticket, and immediately went for his radio, as if to summon help or call for the police;

"We've got a dodger. Pretending to be dead by the looks of him!" he shouted into the mouthpiece whilst simultaneously, and quite violently, shaking the unfortunate David. O'nad interrupted the guard and explained the situation stating that David was an actor, en route to an important audition for a part in Holby City, and that he was merely 'living' his intended role in a way all good 'method actors' do. The guard seemed impressed with this and O'nad issued him with the relevant tickets for David and the others.

"Just one thing sir" said the guard, "You'll have to move that plank of wood, it's blocking the aisle, and we wouldn't want anyone to actually hurt themselves on it now, would we?" O'nad nodded in agreement; at this Heinny produced a rather vicious looking pocket knife and began carefully chipping away at the timber. Julia watched in awe as the adept baboon began whittling away at David's wooden appendage.

By 13:40 the front carriages of the enlarged train had reached the outskirts of the sprawling metropolis of London, though they were actually still in Wales. Heinny had skilfully sawn off a large chunk of wood and begun to carve away the letters 'S,T,N and U' into the remaining end of the plank embedded in David's skull. Julia had repositioned herself into one of the front carriages and listened intently to B'stard and Anul as they plotted their heinous activities.

"Do we have sufficient leeks Master?" asked Anul,

"Oh yes Anul, we have more than enough for the purpose, however we could always stop off at Smithfield Market to buy more if needed." replied B'stard.

Upon arrival at London's Kings Cross station O'nad and crew remained on board their carriage until they were certain that B'stard and Anul had alighted from theirs, watching them gather together the army of the dead and lead them towards their intended target.

Carrying a still unconscious David onto the platform and resting him against a pillar, O'nad, Heinny, Julia and Tobias discussed their next step. As they chatted, a smartly dressed businessman, carrying a briefcase and black umbrella, and sporting a typical businessman's bowler hat walked up to the 'resting' David and began to kick him, quite violently, whilst shouting "We'w, fack orf back ap noorf then!" in a typical, if not stereotypical, cockney twang. When he'd said his piece, the smart gentleman simply carried on with his day and walked off along the platform. O'nad and the gang smiled at each other in a way which would suggest they were each thinking 'result!' Julia could not contain her joy at the sight of her husband being kicked. The victim slowly regained consciousness once more, mainly due to the constant stabbing pains in his side and across his face as, one by one, angry cockneys formed an orderly queue to attack the forlorn, and severely bruised, David. Unable to fight back David was quickly rendered unconscious once more by a particularly savage kick to the head from a Mohican wearing cockney punk rocker's Dr Marten boot. The punk uttered something like "Cheeky nowvern cant!" as he wandered off. O'nad and friends did think of intervening to stop the attacks, but thought better of it, given that there were only four of them against a queue which had grown to

# A Crofter's Tale (The REAL Story of The Hartlepool Monkey)

the entire length of the platform. After thirty or so minutes the group had to reconvene to make haste for Westminster, and so O'nad ushered over a security guard to break up the angry throng and free David from a far worse fate than having a six inch nail embedded in his skull. The guard assisted David to his feet and suggested that he should remove his 'hat' which seemed to have been the cause of so much offence to the London locals.

*"It's just a plank of wood!"* uttered David groggily,

*"No worries Guard, we'll see to it that he takes it off immediately"* interjected O'nad, ushering the officer away whilst the others crowded round David, so as to protect him – or at least make it look as though they were protecting him! Sadly this 'protection' was short lived as a nasty and particularly evil looking Pearly Queen by the name of Steve took umbrage at David's plank of wood and launched a vicious attack using a four foot length of 3" Steel pipe. On seeing the approaching venomous looking thug all four of his 'friends' had legged it, leaving David standing alone in the centre of the platform to face the full fury of the sequined queen.

The force of the first blow was sufficient to knock out David's front teeth (upper and lower) without actually coming into contact with them, the second blow – the succour punch – was an upper cut which mashed his ragged, bloodied gums together whilst at the same time lifting David two feet off the ground so that his head took the full impact of the old railway clock as he rose up to meet it, this had the fortunate effect of dislodging the six inch nail and its attached plank of wood from his skull. David's last thought before he blacked out was *"What a fine piece of carving."* It was amazing what one could do with a piece of 3 x 2 rough cut timber. Heinny had expertly crafted a beautiful sign from the cheap pine, he had thought long and hard about what would be the best use for the timber, whilst shortening it so as to reduce its potential to cause injury to others, before plumping for the legend "ALL

COCKNEYS ARE CANTS" (Heinny had used the literal cockney spelling of the word cunts, so as to make it clear what David was trying to convey) as the subject matter for his carving; thus he reduced the overall length of the wood by one foot. Blood now spurted from the hole in David's skull as the others frantically tried to bring him round. Fearing the worst, and feeling the guiltiest, Heinny was the first of the group to call for an ambulance. The removal of the nail must have served to cause some significant damage within the battered remains of David's cranium for he kept momentarily regaining consciousness; each time he did so a little more blood seeped from his brain and he would pass out once more. Eventually he came fully round and immediately launched a blistering attack on his companions,

"It must be the effects of the concussion." offered Julia, recoiling from her husband's verbal tirade.

"You rotten lot. What did you do that for?" squeaked David through bloodied gums and pointing at the delightful carving,

"Oh, David!" said Julia, "It was just a joke. Stop taking everything so seriously!"

"Some fucking Joke!" he replied, standing up shakily.

"Quick, let's get out of here before the ambulance turns up!" said Heinny. With that our quintet hastily left Kings Cross.

## Chapter 26
### *"The Silence of the Lords"*

As B'stard and Anul and their army of dead Welsh people left Kings Cross station it was rapidly approaching 7pm. Rush hour and the end of the day for most normal Londoners, but the start of the day for those in power.

The group of a thousand dead Welshies blended in quite nicely with the late evening rush hour as they made their way up York Way towards Euston Road from Kings Cross. It was roughly three miles to their intended rendezvous. Westminster. The seat of power in the United Kingdom, and throughout it's former Empire, for over eight hundred years.

The group was in no mad rush as their intended victims would be making their own way from their highly paid day jobs – running banks and multinational conglomerates – *"there might even be one or two of them among us now."* thought B'stard and quickly dismissed the thought as most of them were too infirm to stand, let alone walk, and the few that could walk chose not to for fear of being infected by the populace. On they marched to Westminster, Parliament and the first of the two chambers where so much was decided by so few, The House of Lords.

O'nad, Tobias, Heinny and the Snaiths were in close proximity to the marching zombies. Julia having explained what she had heard being uttered by the B'stard and his Sikh friend. Everyone, except for David, knew where they were heading. David had been told, but was forgetting things due to the enormous damage to his skull, and so he kept asking "Are we there yet?" and "Where are we going?" the others ignored him.

Forty minutes later B'stard and his army arrived in Parliament square. According to what Julia had told the others, it had been their intention to storm the front gate and access the chamber through violent means – killing anyone who stood in their way – this turned out not to be the case as security that day was particularly lax. The usually armed guards at the gates of Parliament had been taken away on a staff training day – 'Promoting Customer Satisfaction' and had been replaced with standard 'Court Officials', who were unarmed and unaware of the

# A Crofter's Tale (The REAL Story of The Hartlepool Monkey)

potential threats, not to mention being unaware of their own names.

Posing as a group of tourists (albeit a particularly large, docile and ugly one) the entire army of the dead had been allowed into the public areas of the Parliament building. No attempt had been made to remove the large vegetables each member wielded as B'stard had explained to the 'Court Officials' that it was a minor protest against the Welsh Assembly and that, immediately after their visit, they would be dishing out the leeks to those who deserved them. The official had seemed impressed with this act of charity and allowed them entry without further interrogation.

After being allowed access to the Palace of Westminster no further security was apparent. To their right a sign read "Lords' Chamber" and B'stard indicated to his troops the way forward through St Stephens' Hall and into the Central Chamber, from here the Lords' Chamber was to their right, Commons to their left. So as not to arouse too much suspicion from the non-existent guards B'stard ordered his army to peruse the walls and ceiling of the splendidly decorated central chamber, whilst surreptitiously making their way through the narrow corridor towards the doorway to the chamber. Immediately one thousand zombies began sidling to the right whilst staring at the ceiling and walls, and at the same time making 'Ooh' and 'aah' sounds in mock awe. Within seconds every one of the welsh zombies, menacingly brandishing the finest leeks, was at the doorway to the chamber housing their intended victims.

It was a 'full house' inside the chamber of the Lord's; an important debate on the government's plans to introduce free housing and fuel to the poorest in society was expected to be widely opposed by the wealthy, fat, ignorant and senile old farts. Some of the Conservative members had even been ferried in by NHS air ambulance from their death beds to oppose the socially responsible, but fiscally stupid, legislation. The chamber resembled a care home for the mentally ill. The majority of the Lords sat drooling or foaming at the mouth, whilst the remainder were prostrate on the benches, asleep or dead, or being revived for the purpose of the vote. None of them noticed the stealthily creeping zombies as they entered the chamber from all sides. A nurse, busily changing the incontinence pad of one of the Lords was the first to see the leek wielding zombies,

"My Goodness!" she exclaimed; her last words, as the zombie before her filled her mouth and throat with the mild onion tasting vegetable, jamming it so far down her gullet that she could not get purchase on its shaft in order to extract it and she promptly fell, suffocating, to the floor. The Lord who was having his nappy changed stirred slightly and opened his mouth as if to feed from a bottle, the 'bottle' in this instance, was a thick green and white leek.

The Lord Chancellor, or leader of the Lords, Lord Burly of Pove, sat upon the woolsack at the head of the chamber. At just 94, and therefore the youngest and most active member, he had been given the job of ensuring that the other Lords complied with regulation and tradition, and also that any 'mess' they made was swiftly cleaned up by the chamber attendants; he weakly shouted "Order, order!" to the chaotic scene before him,

*"Here's your order, Sir, isn't it, look you!"* whispered one of the zombies into the ear of Lord Burly, whilst at the same time jamming his long, firm leek swiftly down his victims throat.

Death came swiftly upon the Lords that evening. Within twenty minutes
each and every solitary Lord, whether alive or dead, had been killed, or further killed, in the most gruesome and violent act of vegicide the country had ever witnessed, in fact it was the only act of vegicide ever seen in Britain, and it resulted in the deaths of all seven hundred and forty four peers.

Once each Lord had been 'dealt with', the process began of replacing each Lord with a Welsh Zombie. Amazingly, and despite the enormous loss of blood, no evidence remained of the mass killing within the chamber, this was in the main due to the deep red carpet and seating, though the blockage of certain bleeding orifices with leeks also had a lot to do with the cleanliness of the slaughter. Within minutes of the work being done and the chamber being cleared of the remnants of their Lordships, Anul stepped forward to order his troops to don the traditional ceremonial cloaks and hats of the Lords and take up positions previously occupied by the 'real McCoy'. Anyone now venturing into the chamber would notice that their Lordships were in particularly lively mood – a far cry from the usual snoozing, dozing or dead scene. B'stard knew that their next task would be much more difficult and therefore needed time to plot his treachery.

O'nad and the others waited outside of the parliament building. Knowing full well the plans for mass murder inside both chambers of the historic place, they had decided that it would better serve the British population if their enemies were allowed to conduct their heinous act and rid the country of the greedy, selfish, perverse and scurrilous Members of Parliament and the equally scurrilous and exceptionally inane and pointless Lords. In any case they hadn't yet thought of a means of curtailing the actions of their enemy.

B'stard now donned the traditional garb of the leader of the Lords, ignoring the damp patch on the seat of the gown; obviously some sort of bodily fluid from the late Lord Burly of Pove, though most certainly not blood. Taking his place upon the woolsack 'Lord' B'stard of Minge, as he'd imaginatively titled himself, began shouting his troops to order. To his right stood 'Lord' Anul of Arse, who had taken the role of Chief Whip – for reasons known only to himself, though his colossal perversity might have been a deciding factor.

"Order, Order!" shouted B'stard, silence befell the room instantly. "Thank you, your 'Lordships', thank you very much!" he smiled, "Phase one is over and we have secured our first objective. Soon, members of the 'other place' will take up their seats." he used the terminology he had learnt from years of viewing the Parliament Channel, and remembered that each 'house' never mentioned the other 'house' by name, referring to each other as 'the other place' in a tradition of pointless superstition spanning hundreds of years, "and when they do, we will need to be far more stealthy in our approach to 'taking them out'. They are a lot younger, and potentially therefore, more alive, than our most recent victims. I doubt that our choice of weapon will be much use on them, as they're used to all sorts of leaks!" he sniggered at his own witticism, Anul hissed. "Rather we need to find a more suitable tool, and where better than this place, with their, err sorry, your Lordships' ceremonial swords? My learned Lord Anul here will outline the plans for phase two of our quest whilst issuing each of you with a sword!" Anul was, by this time, doubled over yet again in wanton anticipation of his expected sword issuing. B'stard wondered why it took two hours for Anul to issue the swords, but did not question him, assuming that he was simply instructing each new 'Lord' in the use of their tool.

B'stards' plan was simple, as was B'stard for thinking it could be achieved so easily.

"We will now march upon the other place and order them to capitulate to our immense power. If they do so without a struggle there will be little need for us to utilise our weapons. However, if they do not surrender, then shall we let battle commence. Come, good dead people, let us make for the House of Commons." he stood, immediately followed by his army. B'stard thought it would be a simple task to take out the Members of Parliament. On paper at least, given that there were a thousand of them and only six hundred and fifty nine M.P's, none of whom, to his knowledge, would be armed.

# Chapter 27
*"Members Dismembered"*

Leaving the Lords' Chamber and heading north through a narrow corridor the army eventually came upon the central lobby where they had first entered the building, from there a short walk through another corridor led them into the Commons Lobby, then, directly in front of them lay the doors to the Commons Chamber.

A number of MPs milled around the lobby prior to taking up their seats in the Commons chamber. Despite having such a large number of MP's the chamber could only seat just over four hundred of them, the rest had to make use of the stairways and carpeted floor of the room. The MPs awaited news from the other place as to the outcome of their vote on the social housing and fuel reform and, as it was such an important vote, with TV cameras and photo opportunities aplenty, every one of the six hundred and fifty nine members had gathered to hear the outcome.

Waiting in the corridor before entering the lobby stood B'stard, Anul and the cloaked Army of the Dead. Only when the final MP had entered the Chamber and the huge wooden door had closed behind him did the army make their move. Racing across the lobby floor, the Charge of the Dead Brigade had begun. Anul performed the usual role of Black Rod, quite apt given his racial make up and propensity to utilise his 'rod' at every given opportunity, and hammered three times on the door to the chamber, at which point the MP's within allowed entry to the one who would reveal the result of the Lords' vote. It had been hoped, by the majority within, that the result would come in in time for the ten o'clock news bulletins so that a major victory for the government could be announced, live, to the eagerly waiting country. Sadly, due to the slow pace of the issuing of swords by Anul, the news bulletins had passed and the cameras had been switched off. There would be no live announcement, nor would the cameras capture the historic and bloody events about to unfold.

The moment that the heavy oak doors opened, B'stard and Anul both shouted *"Charge!"* and with swords slashing to and fro, cutting into the flesh of the MP's closest to them, they hacked their way into the Commons Chamber. Within moments the entire chamber was circled and the zombies stood with swords at the ready, eager to begin their bloodbath. B'stard spoke up first to his bloodthirsty troops.

"Patience, my Lords, your time will come soon." then, unceremoniously, he shoved the Speaker off his chair with his sword, piercing the unfortunate members' rib cage and slicing his heart in two, and stood before the mumbling, terrified MP's. Once more a silence fell upon the room as B'stard spoke.

"Allow me to introduce myself" he said, "I am Lord B'stard of Minge, and the delightful fellow currently holding your Prime Ministers' testicles is my learned, and leaning, friend Lord Anul of Arse. The others you see around you are the new Lords of this land, and I am its new leader." with that he nodded to Anul, who quickly and calmly sliced off the head of the Prime Minister, his lifeless body fell to the cream carpeted floor, blood spurting from the cleanly cut neck. Anul held aloft the fallen leaders head and flung it at the Chancellor of the Exchequer, snapping his neck in the process, killing him instantly. The remaining members in the chamber began to scream and, panicking, made for the doors where they were met by the swords yielded by the new 'Lords'. B'stard shouted above the mêlée.

"Silence! Silence!" the furore continued unabated by B'stards demands for calm, then, remembering the pomposity of

# A Crofter's Tale (The REAL Story of The Hartlepool Monkey)

the debating chamber, he shouted "Order! Order!" Immediately there was silence, though some of the female members could still be heard snivelling, and the chamber came to order for its new leader.

"Thank you; now, let's debate my next action. This has been a military coup on one of the most respected governments of the world. It being so easily completed will prove to the world that, if Britain can be taken over, then every government in the world must surely quake at my presence. You now have two choices; no harm will come to those among you who join us on our quest for world power, for those who choose not to, well, they will die, right here, right now. It's a simple choice, for I know that you are simple folk. What's it gonna be?" he laughed insanely.

Being politicians, and therefore self centred egotists, the majority of the remaining MP's tried the political approach of pretence, pretending to be on the side of the leader, in this case the bad guys, whilst all along plotting to overthrow the evil regime. The most recent example of such political skulduggery was the overthrow of Mrs Thatcher back in 1990. B'stard considered himself to be a good judge of character, having worked for most of his life, in a voluntary capacity, as leader of the Order of The Scrotum; he was well versed in such sycophantic behaviour and instantly ordered those displaying said characteristics to be immediately slaughtered over the despatch boxes.

Half an hour after the coup six hundred and fifty two of the six hundred and fifty nine MP's had been so despatched. Of the remaining seven members, four were Labour front benchers and three were of Liberal Democrat persuasion; no Conservatives remained as B'stard, quite rightly, asserted that they were all just too smarmy and false to be of any use to him.

Phase three of his plan was now discussed among his army and new MP's. This was to be the phase which saw him extract ultimate power; removal, by fair means or foul, of the monarchy.

Unbeknown to B'stard however this was to be the move which would lead to the biggest confrontation so far, the confrontation with O'nad, and payback time for Tobias Wat.

# Chapter 28
## *"Queens Save The Queen"*

It had taken a little over four hours for B'stard and Anul, together with their Army of the Dead, to overthrow both houses of parliament; a further two hours to secure the support of the Greater London Police Commissioner, and now they were ready to march to their next rendezvous with chaos.

In the intervening hours since following B'stard's Army to Westminster, O'nad, Heinny, Tobias and the Snaiths had secreted themselves in a small, all night café, just off Parliament Square. From there they could see the Palace of Westminster and, if they tried hard enough, could hear the screams and cries of the murderous acts being conducted within the ancient walls. Police sirens wailed and blue lights flashed as emergency services were summoned to the building though strangely, no armoured response was called in and after a few hours the police were called away.

In this time O'nad's crew wracked their brains trying to figure out an adequate response to B'stards bloody campaign. It was Heinny who came up with the plan.

"How about that Pearly Queen guy?" he said.

"Oh, come now Mr Himmler, do you really think some sequinned homosexual can sort out B'stard and his gang?" responded O'nad haughtily.

"Well, no," replied Heinny, "not on his own, but this is London, there are hundreds, if not thousands, of those button stitchers here; and what's more they're all fiercely loyal to Her Majesty!"

O'nad pondered the thought for a while before announcing his utter agreement with his monkey friend.

"But where do we find a thousand Pearly Kings and Queens at two in the morning?" he asked; everyone shrugged their shoulders in bewilderment.

"Well," uttered David, speaking for the first time since they arrived, "What about the East End?"

"What about it?" said Heinny dismissively;

"Well, look over there." said David pointing to a large mobile billboard parked at the side of the road. Everyone present nearly soiled themselves in joy as they stared at the brightly coloured poster;

*"Jellied Eels Productions Proudly present*
*The 20th Annual, all night, Pearly King and Queen Ball,*
*The Queen Vic Arena, Walford.*
*Tonight!*
*Special Guest Star – Tommy Stoole*
*Thousands Expected for a good old Cockney Knees up!"*

"What luck!" exclaimed Julia excitedly;

"What luck, indeed." said O'nad. The group quickly made their way to Walford via the night bus service, ensuring first that David was again rendered unconscious for the journey. The rendering being issued with gusto by Julia.

On arrival in Walford our heroes found the Queen Vic Arena by following a group of Pearly Kings, though from the way they were walking, O'nad assumed that they must be 'queens' if truth be known. Once inside the Arena they quickly summoned one of the organisers and explained their plight and the potential threat to the monarchy. The organiser, a particularly camp and feeble looking man, quickly rallied the support of all those present by announcing the news of the attack on the government and the threat to Her Majesty, over the public address system – interrupting Tommy Stoole singing 'Half a Tuppence!' – within minutes everyone there had 'signed up' to support the Royal Family and began making their way, arms linked and singing 'Knees up Muvver Brahn', across Westminster Bridge and on towards Buckingham Palace.

At that precise moment B'stard and Anul and the army of the dead set off from the Palace of Westminster to make their way towards The Mall. The convergence of the two armies seemed inevitable, and so it was proved at the Queen Victoria Monument at the head of The Mall.

The Battle of Buttons and Leeks, as it became known in history, was to be the bloodiest battle seen in London for over a month. The police were powerless to curtail the bloody activity and stood by as a thousand Welsh zombies and fifteen hundred bejewelled Queens clashed, quite alarmingly, in front of Buckingham Palace.

The carnage which took place that morning made Hannibal Lector's crimes look like common assault. The brutality of the slaying, from both parties, was, quite literally, barbaric; heads lopped off, limbs torn from torso's, spines severed, necks broken, eyes gouged, ears ripped off, hair pulled, sequins loosened or, worse still, ripped off, faces scratched and shins kicked. No one seemed able to intervene to stop the bloodbath. The Pearly Queens had brought back up in the form of a seamstress named Nigel, but not even he could stem the massive loss of mother of pearl. The zombies, fuelled by the hate whipped up by B'stard and Anul used their swords to good effect, no stitch was left unpicked. The Pearly Queens, in response, and whilst singing 'My Old Man's a Dustman', fought back with needles and thread, stitching up their victims lips, and other orifices, before slicing off their heads with crimping scissors; some of the more forward thinking Queens had purchased K-Tel Stitch-a-Matiks for this purpose, others got by with just their Knitting needles and wool bags;

After almost two hours bloodshed, and embroidery, the battle was won. The victors were the Pearly Kings & Queens of good old London Town. Their enemies, the Welsh zombies, lay decapitated on the streets of the surrounding battlefield known as The Mall. Although it is a well-known fact (to those who follow the writings relating to the 'horror genre' of zombie stories) that the only way to 'kill' a zombie is by means of decapitation this fact was not known to our heroes the 'Pearly Kings & Queens'. We can assume, therefore, that their actions were born out of 'looking out for your own' and that this form of retribution was 'common place' in the streets of London (certainly within the chimes of Bow Bells) and probably a sensible 'zero tolerance' approach. None-the-less the punishment meted out by the fervent loyalists was both apt and welcome.

Of the one thousand zombies that began their assault on the capital only three or four managed to escape with their 'deaths' (that is to say they escaped with heads in tact and still attached to their spinal columns, and as such preserved their zombified status). These surviving zombies simply wandered off into the surrounding streets where they can still be found today by any unsuspecting visitor to the capital who attempts to seek directions. Note to reader: If you find yourself lost in London ask a 'local' for directions. If your question is answered or greeted with either utter disdain, a shrug of the shoulders, an unfathomable verbal ranting, or you are simply ignored, then you will know you have encountered a true Londoner; if, however, you're answered in a civil manner, and given the correct route to your destination, by a person with a strong Welsh accent you will know that you have encountered one of the surviving members of B'stards' once glorious 'Army of The Dead'.

But what of B'stard and Anul……?

O'nad and company had, throughout the entire battle, been brave enough to stand well clear of the ensuing carnage, instead choosing to observe from a remote position; as was the time honoured tradition of generals when leading their troops to sure and certain ~~death~~ victory. Their approach was not unique for B'stard and Anul had also decided to follow tradition. After all it was the honourable thing to do – Dulce Et Decorum Est, Pro Patria Mori.

Leaving the Pearly Kings & Queens to their well earned victory, which involved them disembowelling their victims and 'jellying their entrails' (to be served up with lashings of mashed potato and Watney's Bleeding Red Barrel, and, curiously, a hint of Leek which was in abundance in London at that time)

O'nad and friends followed B'stard and Anul as they slinked off, heads bowed and dejected. However a quick headcount, by Heinny, revealed that there was an extra person within their midst as they hastened to follow the B'stard and his Sikh cohort.

"Stop!" cried Heinny and the rest of his colleagues dutifully did so (not least Julia who was, by now, a consummate expert in the field of dutifulness).

"What is it?" asked O'nad.

"We've got some company." replied Heinny as he pointed out the 'sixth' member of the group.

"Christ! It's Tommy Stoole!" said David.

"Who?" responded Tobias. With that David proceeded to burst into the refrain from 'Half a Tuppence', all of which was lost on Tobias who had, after all, been dead for the past 200 years and may be forgiven for not knowing who Tommy Stoole was. However, given that Tommy has been performing for at least 200 years (or at least it feels like it) this was in no way mitigation for Tobias' ignorance.

# A Crofter's Tale (The REAL Story of The Hartlepool Monkey)

"Aaaww whyyte!" shrieked Tommy in his loveable chirpy cockney chappie character twang. "Now bordy storps me fram singing arf a Tuppence, not least a banch a zombies and their disrespeckfal mites".

Julia, being a Londoner herself, though certainly not cockney, quickly came to the rescue and translated for her friends.

"I think he's upset that he was cut short in his rendition of the famous ditty 'half a Tuppence'".

"Ask him what he wants will you?" asked O'nad. Julia did as was asked and Tommy replied "Who's respoorrrnsabal then? Cos am ganna do em owver like a kippa." as he asked this he brandished a machete which he'd previously had secreted about his person, smiled a toothy smile and gave a crafty wink.

Not wishing to provoke the four foot three inch psychopath O'nad replied "B'stard, it was B'stard and his vile partner Anul".

"Wryte, where are they then? Ah'll teech them sammannas!" Tommy asked.

Not wanting to look a gift horse in the mouth our friends decided that Tommy Stoole could prove to be useful in their confrontation with B'stard and Anul. Things would probably get rather nasty during their imminent 'end game', and there was a good chance that one of the group could be injured or, worse still, be killed. Using Tommy as an initial 'forward offensive' might get them what they wanted without the need for further casualties. With this in mind Tommy was immediately conscripted into the 'gang' and given his first orders – to kill Mister Dirty B'stard and Anul Abu-Sar.

Tommy and the gang followed B'stard and Anul through the streets until the pair finally came to a stop beside a particularly filthy looking 'Jellied Eel' stall. Tommy seized his opportunity and ran, headlong, towards Anul who was hunched over (more than he'd ever been to date) tying his shoe laces. Tommy Steel thrust the steel of his steely machete into the ribs of Anul, all the time

# A Crofter's Tale (The REAL Story of The Hartlepool Monkey)

screaming and shouting cockney diatribe at the unsuspecting victim. "Bugger!" gasped Anul.

"It's the larst baggering you'll be gettin ma freynd!" shouted Tommy. Tommy obviously knew nothing of Anul's past, sexually deviant, misdemeanours and so whilst he could indeed promise this would be his last buggering, he had no way of knowing quite how many buggerings the Asian deviant had had in the past. Within seconds the Sikh was no more. His lifeless body lay twisted and arched on the roadside next to the 'Jellied Eel' stall. Members of the public (other Londoners), who had clearly witnessed the attack, chose simply to stride over Anul's body as if he wasn't there. B'stard made good his escape behind a nearby wheelie bin, though this did not go unnoticed by Heinny, who maintained a steely look out for Tommy.

"One dahn, one to go!" said Tommy as he wiped the blood from his trusty weapon. O'nad and the others, wishing to maintain the momentum of Tommy's actions, stood and jeered him on.

"Come on Tommy, come on Tommy!" they shrieked. Heinny then silently pointed out B'stard's hiding place to him before adding "Go get him Tommy."

B'stard, who had recently lost his mighty Army at the hands of a bunch of 'queens' and, more recently his second in command, crouched motionless as the menacing figure of Tommy Stoole loomed towards him (in as much as a four foot three inch person can loom). At this point, and for reasons known only to him self, B'stard decided he would try to reason with the pint sized popular entertainer and he stood.

"Come now Mr Stoole. There's no need for all this upset. I'm sure there's a way we can come to some gentleman's agreement, reasonably and rationally. One that need not lead to any unwanted act of violence." with that he thrust Heinny's gooly case and testicle (the right one, as in opposite of left) on the ground in front of him; Tommy paused momentarily, as if to suggest that B'stard was actually getting through with his attempted reason and

# A Crofter's Tale (The REAL Story of The Hartlepool Monkey)

rationale, he glanced at the dried up skin and its strange, mangled orb. B'stard's confidence at seeing his would be assailant pause would, however, be short lived. What B'stard failed to singularly note was that Tommy Stoole was a Londoner, a cockney, and as such the words 'reason' and 'rational' knew no place in his vocabulary; deeply offended at being spoken to in this way (what with the use of such flowery words 'reason' and 'rational') Tommy became incensed. Julia sensed the incensement within Tommy and instinctively knew what was coming next. Tommy lunged towards B'stard with only one thing in mind – murder. Equally instinctively Julia knew what B'stard's next move would be. She observed B'stard thrusting his outstretched palms back and forth and readying his lips for the incant that would make him invisible to his foe. Without a care for her own safety she jumped upon the back of B'stard, holding his arms tight with her thighs as she clamped her legs around his midriff. Before B'stard had chance to utter the words which would secure his safety Julia clamped her hands around his mouth. B'stard fell, forcibly, silent whilst his arms (specifically his palms) were rendered useless. Tommy seized his opportunity and thrust his weapon towards B'stard. Because Julia had mounted B'stard and, as a result, there was an obvious struggle during which Tommy's weapon made contact with B'stard's face rather than it's intended target (his heart) Tommy struck once more in an effort to nail him once and for all. Again the weapon made contact with B'stard's face. The ensuing screams from B'stard startled Julia and she relaxed her grip. This was sufficient for B'stard to throw Julia from his back.

"My eyes, my eyes!" screamed B'stard. "I'm blind, I cannot see!" he further screamed. It was now clear where the blows, struck by Tommy Stoole, had landed. B'stard then stood upright and resumed his outstretched palm position. Heinny knew what was coming next and grabbed the machete from Tommy Stoole's hands (particularly small hands). What had looked like a machete to our heroes turned out to be a potato peeling knife (it's a question of scale). Heinny, armed with potato peeling knife, lunged towards the blinded B'stard as he was uttering the words "Just like that!" Heinny grabbed at B'stard's hands, which by now had disappeared along with the rest of his body. None-the-less Heinny had B'stard in his grasps and, feeling his way over B'stard's body (in a necessary way and not one that would suggest room for innuendo) grabbed at B'stard's hand. With a cut and a slash (well quite a few cuts slashes and hacks) Heinny proceeded to hack off the hand of B'stard. Twenty minutes later B'stard, despite his pleas for mercy, had lost his left hand. Another twenty minutes later, again despite continued pleas for leniency and mercy, B'stard lost his second hand (that is his right hand and not something that is 'used' or to be found on the face of a watch). By now the screams of horror were frightful and unending; Julia slapped her husband hard across the face in an attempt to break his hysteria, instantly the screams stopped. Heinny, by now exhausted and sweating profusely, released his grip on B'stard and fell to the floor. B'stard also fell silent. It is not sure whether he also fell to the floor as he remained, of course, invisible to the others.

With his work seemingly done and another West End show to star in within the hour, Tommy Stoole wandered off towards the Theatre, as he did so the others heard him singing quietly to himself "Whoa, crash bang wallop, wot a pictcher, wot a pictcher wot a fotagrarph.." and as his voice, and tap dancing feet, faded into the distance he was seen no more (more's the pity).

Our group stood besides Heinny and helped him to his feet. B'stard's whimpering could be heard despite him not being seen. He was still obviously in the near vicinity. Then, to everyone's surprise B'stard spoke once more. His words were to prove futile, and were to be met with howls of derisive laughter.

"Just like that!" he declared. Again and again he repeated the words intended to make him visible again, but to no avail. The words that were once his strength were now his curse for B'stard was now unable to make himself visible again as he lacked the means, or rather, the palms, to do so. To compound things for B'stard not only was he invisible but he was also blind, forever destined to wander the earth in limbo but, in the first instance, the East End of London.

The last that was known of B'stard was that he was heard, by our heroes, bumping into things and cursing all the way down the street on which his fate had been sealed. His murmurings slowly fading away as he distanced himself from O'nad and company until his voice could be heard no more.

Victory was complete. B'stard and his evil henchman Anul were no more. Britain was once again safe, as was the world. Our heroes had won the battle with the help of the Pearly Kings & Queens and Tommy Stoole, and saved the Queen to boot, though why they would want to boot her is unknown; Heinny got his ball sac back and David and Julia Snaith were divorced six months later, paving the way for the first baboon / human marriage; O'nad and Toby were honoured by the Queen and tied the knot in a civil ceremony two days after the battle (Well, O'nad tied it) and they all lived happily ever after.

All that is except for David who, after enduring horrendous head injuries during our tale, suffered bouts of severe depression for the next two years, eventually deciding to end it all by a method sure to kill him slowly but decisively.

Finding a suitable vehicle he stood for a while, as if in prayer, and then thrust his bent elbow into the toughened glass of the drivers door window, it shattered into a thousand pieces, the fragmented glass glinting like diamonds in the evening sun; without bothering to clear away any of the shards from the seat, David climbed in, adjusted the seat so that his legs could stretch out fully, closed the door behind him, and waited. He waited for a full twenty minutes and then it dawned on him. The full realisation of his wasted years; how his aversion to all things automotive (excepting, perhaps the Robin Reliant) had led him to force his wife into a three week cart ride from London to Hartlepool, which had, in turn, brought her and that fucking baboon closer and closer; had caused her to hate him to the point of wanting him dead, which eventually led to their divorce, this aversion and fear which had now spectacularly failed to manifest itself so that he could end it all.

His phobia had been unwarranted; he felt no ill effects on entering the vehicle. Snapping back to the present David's realisation became a ray of hope for him; at last he could see a brighter future and, smiling to himself for the first time in years he made to get out of the car.

"An where d'ya fink you're going, you nonce? Bin touchin a dog's 'arris ave ya? Wew not mine you aint!"

David turned to face the voice now booming at him. He was still smiling as the first blow from Tommy Stoole's machete sliced his skull in two.

As for B'stard, well he's still out there, somewhere, but not even he knows where that somewhere is!

## FIN.

Printed in Great Britain
by Amazon